THE BRONZE CHRYSANTHEMUM MYSTERY
by Sheena Porter

Illustrated by Shirley Hughes

Ellie, Roger and Jane were wondering what birthday present they should get for their mother when they met a gypsy with a basket of beautifully carved wooden chrysanthemums for sale. They bought them and thought they had solved their immediate problem. After the chrysanthemums had been placed in the window, other problems seemed to arise in the family. A strange man, looking like a mouse, tried to buy the chrysanthemums, then the window pane was expertly cut, but worst of all, Angus, their old dog, disappeared. Ellie insisted it was because of the chrysanthemums, but even the police didn't agree with her until the window pane was cut again and the bronze chrysanthemum was the only one stolen. The police were really looking for silver stolen from the Hall in the village and Ellie's problems sounded like nonsense to them. Ellie added things up and, like a good detective should, explained the clues that led her to the solution of the mystery.

Classification and Dewey Decimal: Fiction (Fic)

About the Author:

SHEENA PORTER enjoyed an outdoor life in the small town in England where she was born. She worked as a children's librarian before deciding to try her own hand at writing. Miss Porter has lived in six different countries and is interested in animals, archaeology, music and reading.

THE BRONZE
CHRYSANTHEMUM
MYSTERY

Sheena Porter

Illustrated by

Shirley Hughes

1968 FIRST CADMUS EDITION
THIS SPECIAL EDITION IS PUBLISHED BY ARRANGEMENT WITH
THE PUBLISHERS OF THE REGULAR EDITION
D. VAN NOSTRAND COMPANY, INC.
BY
E. M. HALE AND COMPANY
EAU CLAIRE, WISCONSIN

Library of Congress Catalog Card No. 65-17041

This edition lithographed in U.S.A. by Wetzel Brothers, Inc., Milwaukee, Wisconsin

To
MY FATHER
and to
JAN

Because this book was first published in Britain, spelling and punctuation differ from what is the custom in the United States. Following are the explanations of a few words in the text which may be unfamiliar to American readers:

ash-keys—the seed of the ash tree

dandy-clock—a dandelion when the seed-heads are ready to disperse

haws—hawthorn berries

pikelets—the same as crumpets or English muffins

ride—a lane cut in a forest

CONTENTS

Baker's Half-dozen

ELLIE WAS STANDING on the top bar of the fence, holding on to the ash-tree, and feeling the wind tugging at her
hair. She'd lost one hair-ribbon in the morning, anyway,
and Roger was using the other one to mend the handle of
his basket. Now that Ellie had her hair loose, she was one
of Boadicea's warriors and the swaying branches of the
ash-sapling in her hand were the reins of her chariot. She
closed her eyes to see the wild horses in front of her, and

nearly fell on her nose as Roger grabbed her by the ankle.

'What do you think you're doing, then? Even you ought to know that blackberries don't grow on ash-trees!' said Roger.

Ellie jumped off the fence over his head. 'I thought that ash-keys would make a change with apples.'

'Well, I'd rather have blackberries myself and we've only half filled the second basket so far. Get a move on.'

'Yes,' said Ellie, 'I truly will now, because it's three already. Where's Jane got to?'

'She was haring up the Bewley road the last time I saw her. I think that she was trying to reach the hedge by Totty's brook before we did,' said Roger. 'I'll race you.'

He won quite easily, although Ellie was a year older, because she ran on the grass verge, this time being one of Boadicea's horses, a red mare.

When they saw Jane she was looking slightly guilty, and her lips were blue. Roger peered into the basket.

'You've been eating them,' he said.

'I know. I blew on a dandy-clock and it said tea-time. Besides, I only had one out of every five,' she explained, peering into the basket too.

'It is tea-time, more or less,' said Ellie, 'or it will be, by the time we're home. Let's pick fast for twenty minutes by my watch, which will be half past three, which means that it will be ten to four by the right time. Then we'll go back for the bikes.'

They moved slowly up the hedge in silence, with Roger beside Jane to keep an eye on her. Then they turned and walked back to the Bewley cross-roads where they had left their bikes hidden in the hedge bottom.

Jane saw the dog first, and went straight across the grass

to speak to him. He sniffed her outstretched hand diffi-
dently, but cautiously wagged his tail and stayed still. She
rubbed him behind his ears, and he looked contented.

'What's happened to it?' said Ellie. 'It looks just like
Wally Smith's wife when she's had her hair permed.'

Jane looked up at her reproachfully.

'Don't be so rude; he'll hear you,' she said. 'He's a
curly-coated retriever. There's a photograph of one in my
dog book.'

Then they saw the man. He was leaning on the field
gate, watching them.

'He's got hair just like the dog,' whispered Ellie, 'but
longer.'

'He's a gipsy,' said Roger. 'He's selling something.'

'No,' said Ellie, 'the men don't sell things out of baskets
like that. It's the women who go round the houses.'

'Well, he's got something there,' said Roger, 'and I don't
see why you think that it's only women who sell things out
of baskets.'

The dog, moving from under Jane's hand, trotted over
the grass to the man, who picked up his basket and came
towards them. Jane stood up rather quickly, because she
wasn't sure whether she liked him. He had on a brown shirt
with the sleeves rolled up, and the sort of green corduroy
trousers that go grey when you sit down in them.

'I hope that you're having better luck than what I am,'
he said in a friendly way, looking at their two large
baskets.

Ellie smiled at him, and Jane tickled the dog under his
chin.

'What are you selling then?' asked Roger. 'We've only
got blackberries here.'

'Well, I'm way behind the times, I reckon,' said the man, and slipped the sack from the top of his basket as he spoke. 'Dare say it's my own fault that I've so many left. Folks seem to want everything washable these days.'

He put the basket on the grass, and they saw that what he had there was a large bunch of wood-shaving chrysanthemums. They were beautifully made, and stained tawny-orange and pale yellow, crimson and white, pink and bronze.

'Oh, how pretty they are!' said Ellie, picking out a crimson one, and looking at it against the blue sky.

'Roger,' she went on, 'come here a minute.'

'What is it?' asked Roger, moving away with her. 'Who said he wasn't selling things?'

Ellie ignored this.

'Have you any money?' she asked, unbuckling the saddle-bag of her bike, and getting her fingers caught up in the long grass.

'What, here?' asked Roger, feeling in his one remaining pocket. All his others had been neatly stitched up by Mrs Leyland, because of what he kept in them. 'Yes, just ninepence. What do you want it for?' he asked.

'Good,' said Ellie. 'I've got half a crown. That should be enough.'

'What *for*?' said Roger.

'That's three and threepence, isn't it?' replied Ellie. 'For Mother's birthday present, of course. Don't you remember how she was talking last week about those wooden chrysanthemums? She said that all our local gipsies seem to bring round, these days, is plastic clothes-pegs and those funny twig-things with coloured plastic bobbles stuck on them.'

'Good idea,' said Roger. 'I should think we could get about two dozen for three and threepence.'

'Goodness no!' exclaimed Ellie. 'It'll be more like half a dozen.'

As they went back they heard Jane chattering to the man, telling him how long they had lived in Castle Tambley.

'He knows where everyone lives, Ellie,' she said, and turned to him. 'How do you know that?' she asked.

The man looked down at his basket.

'Well, I do reckon that I know most of these villages around the hill,' he replied.

'Where do you live then?' asked Jane.

'Oh, here and there you know; I move around a bit.' The man got to his feet as he spoke, and picked up the sack, to replace it over the flowers.

'Please wait a moment,' said Ellie. 'We'd like to buy some of your chrysanthemums for our mother. How many can we have for three and threepence?'

He put his basket on the grass again.

'You pick out six, and we'll see how they look,' he said.

This proved to be easier said than done, as it involved some heated discussion between Jane and Roger.

While this was going on, the man found a wilted cigarette in his trouser pocket, and walked back over the grass to the field gate. The dog got up with a sigh to follow him.

'Where's he gone?' asked Roger, without looking round.

Ellie peered up through the tangle of her hair.

'Over to the hedge. He's got a lighter out of his coat pocket,' she said.

'Hasn't got a coat. You know, you look like an Afghan hound,' replied Roger, ungraciously.

'Yes, he has. It's hanging on the gate-post. At least an Afghan hound is a noble animal; you look more like a Peke, with that nose.'

The gipsy lit his cigarette and leant over the gate, smoking and whistling through his teeth.

'We must have these two lovely rusty ones,' said Ellie. 'They are both exactly the same colour.'

'Oh, no,' said Jane. 'We must have six different colours. It will make the bunch look bigger.'

Ellie knew what she meant, and between them they picked out a pink, a yellow, a bronze, a white, a crimson, and a tawny-orange.

'I think that these six are the best,' said Ellie, gathering them together.

Jane was rooting round in the bottom of the basket, making sure, and found another bronze chrysanthemum almost hidden under the newspaper that lined it. She pulled it out, and it was a bigger flower than the one they already had. She gave it to Ellie in exchange, and straightened the rest of the flowers in the basket. Roger produced a yellow ribbon from his one pocket and tied the bunch up with a surprisingly neat bow.

Jane looked at it.

'That's just the same colour as Ellie's hair-ribbon,' she said.

Ellie looked at it.

'That *is* Ellie's hair-ribbon,' she said. 'Where did you get that from?'

'I picked it up in the road. I thought it might come in handy for something or other,' Roger answered.

The retriever came up then and wagged his thin tail hard all over their legs. Ellie and Roger moved rapidly aside to give him wagging room. He jumped up to put his fore-paws on Jane's shoulders and lick her nose. She sat down rather hard and fast and began to giggle. The dog jumped over her, and then stood on her and began to bark.

'Them two's making a deal of noise between them,' said the man. 'Made up your minds then, have you?'

'Yes, thank you,' said Ellie. 'Is it all right to have these?'

'Surely,' he said. 'And another one will make it seven— baker's half-dozen, as you might say, with one for luck.'

He picked out a golden-yellow one as he spoke and gave it to Roger, who managed to work it into the bunch with-out undoing his good bow.

'Thanks very much,' he said. 'That's a beauty.'

'Quite all right,' said the man. 'A pleasure.'

He took the three and threepence from Ellie, and picked up his basket.

'Good-bye, dog,' said Jane. 'Mind you keep on the path.'

'There isn't a path, you goon,' objected Roger.

'He knows what I mean,' said Jane, and waved to the man, who was climbing over the field gate. 'Good-bye, gipsy.'

'What a lucky thing that we met him,' said Ellie in an

upside-down voice, as she bent to pull her bicycle from the hedge. 'Just in the nick of time. I was going to collect those handkerchiefs from Betty's shop on our way through the village, but she won't mind if we don't have them.'

'Good,' said Jane, 'I haven't any money.' She bounced her small bicycle over the grass to the road.

'We'll never be able to ride, you know.' Ellie was worried, because it was suddenly a quarter past four by her watch, and therefore twenty-five minutes to five by the right time.

'If we have to walk, it'll be past six by the time we're home,' she said.

'All you need is organization,' said Roger, unbuckling Ellie's saddle-bag. He laid the chrysanthemums straight across it, and just managed to get the buckle into the last hole. Then he pulled two polythene bags from his pocket, emptied the blackberries into them and placed them, rather squashed by now, in his saddle-bag and Ellie's bike basket.

'Roger Leyland, master packer,' he said, hooked a basket on to each shoulder, and rode off in pursuit of Jane, looking, so Ellie thought to herself, rather like an American football player with his padding on.

She didn't hurry, but caught them up anyway half a mile farther on. Roger was having to wait for Jane because, as she explained, she had to pedal round three times to his once. Ellie and Roger took a handlebar each and gave her a tow, something highly illegal, but highly satisfying to Jane.

When they rode into Castle Tambley and past the church, the clock showed ten minutes past five on its blue and gilded face, freshly painted and the joy of the Vicar's heart.

'Exactly right for tea,' said Roger, as they wheeled their bikes into the garage. 'What shall we do with the flowers?'

'I think that they will be safe here,' replied Ellie, and shut them inside an old bureau which stood against the wall, awaiting conversion into a kitchen cabinet.

Jane opened the back door and a small yellow dog exploded into the garden.

'Go away,' said Daddy, who was sitting at the kitchen table. 'Go away again. I was going to eat *all* the apple snow and cream.'

2

Cobwebs and Chrysanthemums

ELLIE HAD SET herself to wake early. Roger was always trying to do it, but now resigned himself to the fact that some time during the small hours of the morning he switched himself off.

Ellie was awake all over as soon as she opened her eyes. She crawled down to the bottom of the bed, and stood upon it to look out of the window. Her room was long and thin, squeezed up in the roof of the house with a little gable window high on each end wall. Ellie didn't mind this at all. It made her feel more alone when she was reading, and more dry and warm when it was blowing hard and raining at the same time, and she was in bed.

There was one sparrow sitting on the wooden cross-piece of the gable. Under his stubby tail Ellie saw High-comb Hill, floating above the river mist. She loved it like that because, if you stared at it long enough, it seemed as though the hill itself was moving, sailing majestically into the morning under the still clouds. She focused her eyes again, and knew that the hill was as usual, and it was the clouds that were drifting in a sky that was beginning to be blue.

She went quietly and steeply down her own private flight of stairs, just wide enough for one narrow person, and opened the door into the kitchen.

Angus was watching to see who came in, and when he saw that it was Ellie, thumped his tail heavily in his bed. At the moment this was a cardboard box labelled in red letters *British Bacon Is Best*, and Roger had added in red chalk *for British Borders*, because Angus was a Border terrier.

Ellie put the kettle over a medium-sized jet, looked at the clock, and turned the gas low instead. It was earlier than she had thought. She opened the door wide to let the evening before out, and today's morning in. No one ever locked their doors at Tambley.

She scratched the top of Angus's head and he stretched all four legs out stiffly and arched his back.

'You ought to come out; it would do you good you know,' said Ellie.

He curled up again and closed his eyes. Now that he was thirteen, older than Ellie herself, he refused to have any exercise or conversation before what he considered to be a reasonable getting-up time. Ellie fetched a corner of cheese from the pantry and he ate it with his eyes closed.

She moved Daddy's pipe, a new bootlace, and a battered

rubber ball from the kitchen window-seat, and went round to fetch the chrysanthemums.

They looked so real when she took them out of the old bureau cupboard that she absent-mindedly went to turn the tap on and put them in a jug. She remembered in time, however, and laid them carefully on the window-seat in the thin sunshine.

Then she sorted out her school library book from her satchel, and went down to sit on the log at the bottom of the garden, away from signs of civilization. This was necessary because the book was *The Swiss Family Robinson,* an old favourite of hers.

A quarter of an hour and three chapters later Jane went by towards the currant bushes in a purposeful way.

'Where are you off to, my lass?' asked Ellie in a Robinson voice.

'Oh, there you are then. We wondered where you'd gone. I'm making Mother an extra present, that's all,' replied Jane, walking carefully away over the dewed and shining grass, with a long twig from the privet hedge in her hand.

Ellie closed the book, with a yellow leaf for a book-mark, and went indoors. Roger was making the tea, and threw the kettle-holder at her when she put up her hands in astonishment.

They heard the kitchen ceiling creak twice, as someone got out of bed.

'The back-door side. That's Mother,' said Roger, and hauled himself upstairs by the banister rail to make her get back into bed and wait for her birthday-early cup of tea.

'Although it doesn't seem early at all to me now, Angus,' said Ellie, hearing the boards creak in reverse, and know-

ing that Mother was back in bed. 'Perhaps it's because I've been finding out how to make bottles out of gourds, though. That takes time.'

Roger laid the breakfast then, and Ellie laid the fire and lit it. It was the wrong way about, but Ellie liked the smell of the fire-lighter and building altars with frames of sticks, and Roger liked the smell of the pantry.

Mother exclaimed over the beauty, and the surprise, of the chrysanthemums and Roger explained about meeting the gipsy and his dog yesterday. Daddy wandered out to find the morning paper and Jane wandered in with her extra, and freshly made, present for Mother's birthday.

'It's a cobweb mat to stand the flowers on,' she said, 'and all embroidered with best dew.'

The privet twig had been bent round and tied with string to form a circle, and Jane had stolen all the spiders' webs in the garden, scooping them up to make the middle. Dew shone bright on the top web and showed dimly on all those underneath, and the yellow privet leaves made a scalloped edge to hold them together.

'Thank you, all three and every one,' said Mother. 'I'll put the mat on the mantelpiece for just now.'

'Watch it then,' said Roger, 'or you will have all those poor bereft spiders marching up there to claim their property.'

'It's not only poor spiders that are bereft,' moaned Daddy in a depressed voice, from the door-way.

He held up four long heads of dark blue delphinium, two in each hand. Then he bowed and presented one each to Mother, Ellie, and Jane, and stuck one in the empty milk-bottle on the draining-board.

'But, John, they aren't long enough,' said Mother.

'It's that dratted maggoty paper-boy,' explained Daddy. 'He thinks he's jet-powered instead of pedal-powered. He zoomed up the road making Sputnik noises and hurled the paper over the hedge, straight at me and the delphiniums. I ducked, but the delphiniums didn't have time to.'

'We'll have to find something to put with them then,' said Mother. She fetched two vases from the cupboard. 'Put the chrysanthemums in the sitting-room window in the brown vase, will you, Ellie? Don't throw that yellow ribbon away. It might be useful as a hair-ribbon for you.'

Ellie replied that it already was a hair-ribbon for her, and carried the chrysanthemums through to the front room.

'At least I shan't have to remember to give them fresh water,' said Mother.

'You'll have to remember to dust them instead,' said Roger.

Saturday lunch was always a casual affair. Jane ate hers sitting on the back door-step, where she could feed the stringy ends of the sausages to Angus without anyone noticing. Angus never seemed to mind how stringy they were.

Afterwards they managed to persuade Daddy to give up his usual digestive half-hour, and set off for a long walk to celebrate Mother's birthday.

'Only a slow and peaceful one, mind,' he bargained. 'Remember that I've been working my fingers to the bone these last five weeks, to keep you three in holiday luxury. I'm not strong any more. Angus and I are growing old and feeble together.'

To see if this was true, Jane picked up a thistle in her handkerchief and chased him with it. Angus chased them both, and Daddy pretended to climb a tree in terror.

Mother chose which way they went, so they took the old farm road up Highcomb. Roger didn't usually go that way, because it climbed only slowly in curls and twists, but it was Jane's favourite because it went through two farm-yards.

Half-way up, they sat on the verge to get cool again. Angus chewed the bright green grass in the ditch bottom and made Ellie hungry. She moved down the lane to find a sloe bush, and returned with her hands full.

'You can take your pick now,' she said, and offered her two hands to Mother to choose from. There were black-berries, sloes, a hazel-nut in a velvet shell which wasn't nearly ripe, haws, and four crab-apples. Daddy put the hazel-nut in his button-hole, and ate half a sloe, but stopped because it made his teeth jump.

'Have you noticed the difference in the colour of these haws?' said Ellie. 'Some are blue-red, and some are yellow-red, and some are bright scarlet.'

She bit one and as always was disappointed in the cold-potato taste of it. She threw it at Roger, and it became entangled in his hair.

Jane made a little man out of a crab-apple and a sloe, with twig legs and arms, and put it in Daddy's pocket when he wasn't looking.

'Gussy, come up out of that ditch, you dreadful dog,' said Mother. 'You'll be sick all over the kitchen floor.'

When they reached the top of Highcomb they stood ankle-deep in the warm tussocky grass and looked down over Tambley and across the river to Bewley and the grey cathedral.

'I can see the sun shining on the greenhouse in the school garden,' said Ellie, looking in the opposite direction towards Riddington.

'I can see the cactus in the greenhouse, and the fish in the river,' said Jane. 'Bullies and sticklebacks.'

'You are a terrible fibber, Jane Leyland,' said Roger, and put up his fists ready to defend himself.

Jane withered him with a look. 'I have a vivid imagination, which sometimes leads me to exaggerate. That's what Miss Pilgrim put on my little sheet last term. So I'm not a fibber at all.'

They walked over the flat top of the hill to see if Mr Kennedy's new pond had filled yet. Roger had helped him to dig it on what had seemed to be the two hottest days of the whole summer, and then they had had no rain for four weeks. Now it was half full, and beginning to look more settled and at home.

Jane had been worried in case it should feel empty, and had insisted a fortnight ago on making a special pond-stocking expedition. They had brought to it some crows-foot weed, a root of kingcups, six snails, four little frogs, three smooth brown newts, and one black-crested newt. Ellie was half afraid of this as it looked so like a miniature brontosaurus.

Now, as they stood on the raw brown bank, they saw a brown newt rise to the surface with its tiny hands pressed to its sides. It seemed to be looking up at them curiously while it was treading water, before it turned down again towards the green bottom with a flash of its bright orange and spotted underneath.

'It came up to say thank you, and to show us that it was still here,' said Jane contentedly.

The wispy streamers of cloud were already reflecting the sunset when they entered Tambley again with, as Roger said, their tongues hanging out. Mother expressed the hope that this was only metaphorical, except in the case of Angus, who seemed to have at least half a yard of tongue.

'Good,' said Daddy, seeing their kitchen chimney smoking. 'The fire's still in, so there will be nice hot water to wash in. That gipsy man is certainly clever; those chrysanthemums really do look alive.'

They stood in the road to admire them through the sitting-room window.

'They look so genuine now, because it is chrysanthemum time,' said Mother. 'But what will they look like in the spring?'

'Never mind,' said Roger. 'You can put them in the cupboard then, and we'll buy you some plastic apple-blossom for Christmas!'

'No one needs plastic blossom in Worcestershire, thank goodness,' replied Mother. 'And if you buy me any, then I shall serve you up a plastic plum-pudding for Christmas dinner.'

3

The Mouse-man

'Why is it Saturday again already?' asked Roger of
no one in particular. 'The last week of the holidays always
vanishes into thin air.'

He sat on one end of the kitchen table, polishing shoes
on a newspaper, and Jane was cleaning brasses at the
other end.

'Well, you did work quite hard, didn't you?' replied
Mother. 'I'm sure that Mr Kennedy was very glad of your
help with those last two fields.'

Ellie was sitting on the hearth-rug, beside Angus, sew-
ing on name-tapes.

'I can't see,' she said, stretching her fingers, 'why you
even have to have your name on your socks, Roger. When
is anyone going to get a chance to pinch them? Surely they
don't let you run around bare-foot at Bewley?'

Mother changed the subject quickly, because that of
name-tapes was rather a difficult one with Jane. Roger was
starting his first term at Bewley Boys' Grammar School,
and Jane envied very much the smart red and white name-
tapes that made Roger P. Leyland sound such an important
person.

'I'll finish those off, dear, thank you. Will you go down
to the shop and get some sausages before they're all sold?'
she said.

'Yes, all right,' said Ellie, and picked up the housekeeping purse from the table. 'I'll get some dog biscuits at the same time, and you need some more white cotton and Daddy wants the smallest book of stamps. Come along, Gus, and choose which biscuits you would like.'

The wind was warm and wet, and Ellie felt that she could catch up handfuls of it. It lifted her plaits and thumped them down on her shoulders, and blew Angus's ears up straight, like little sails.

'Coming on for rain, Miss Leyland,' shouted the Vicar's gardener. He was standing on a kitchen chair with no back to it, to clip the vicarage hedge.

Ellie agreed with him, and privately hoped that it would. She loved walking in warm rain, feeling it splashing on her face, and hearing it tapping on the leaves, and sniffing its own particular sweet smell.

She had to pick Angus up and hold him in the village shop. There was a notice on the door that requested that all dogs should be left outside, but Angus had grown rather absent-minded in his old age, so that he forgot what he was standing there for, and went away on his own.

Ellie took her place at the back of the shop and waited while Mr Kennedy bought slug pellets and cigarettes, and Miss Pilgrim, Jane's school-mistress, bought paper handkerchiefs. The refrigerator hummed quietly beside her, and the canary in the back room sang whilst it did so, and fell suddenly silent each time it switched itself off.

Betty smiled at Ellie and passed a broken biscuit across the counter for Angus.

'Nice morning while the rain holds off,' said Mrs Simkin, handing over her grocery list. She lived out on Mr Maitland's estate in the lodge, and her husband was the gamekeeper.

'How's Kenneth today, then? Is he still in bed?' she said.

'I'm afraid so,' said Betty. 'I'm managing to get every-thing done but the deliveries. Will you be able to manage those on your bike in this wind, Mrs Simkin? He shouldn't have got up when he did, you know. The doctor was annoyed with me, but I just couldn't stop him. He felt so much better.'

'Yes,' said Mrs Simkin. 'Bronchitis takes more getting over than you'd think, in my experience. What do you want, Ellie? You serve her first, Betty, and I'll have a sit down.'

Ellie thanked her and shifted Angus over under her other arm, where he twisted and scratched at her in annoyance.

'No, you can't get down yet,' said Ellie, pulling his ears to try to please him. 'Betty doesn't want you paddling mud all over her clean floor, and sniffing at the vegetables.'

Mrs Simkin and Betty laughed at him, because he looked so cross, and Ellie hurriedly picked up her shopping and put the purse back in her pocket, because he hated to be laughed at. She said good-bye, and closed the door care-fully behind her.

As she went up past the church, she noticed a stranger walking in front of her. You always did notice strangers in Castle Tambley, because so few ever came there. There was no through road, as the village lay so close under the hill. Anyone who came in went back the same way.

Even if this hadn't been so, Ellie reflected, she would still have noticed this particular man. Instead of walking straight up the middle of the road, as was normal in Tambley because there was so little traffic, he strolled from one side to the other, peering in everyone's front windows. Ellie rather liked to do this herself, when the lights were on in winter and the curtains not drawn, but she did at least do it unobtrusively.

As she was wondering if the man was just curious or was looking for a house name, the postman came out of Miss Pilgrim's and waved a letter at her.

'I've one here for a Miss Elinor Leyland. Now where do you reckon she lives, Ellie girl?' he asked solemnly.

'Oh Joe, you know perfectly well,' replied Ellie, grinning at him. She studied the writing on her envelope. 'I wonder who this is?'

'Well, best way is to open it, my dear,' suggested Joe, rummaging in his bag for the other letters for the family.

'Oh blow!' said Ellie. 'It's from that pesky new English mistress at school. A reading list, and only one and a half days more holiday. What an optimist!'

Joe handed her a coloured post-card for her mother, and an electricity bill for her father. Ellie thanked him, and continued up the road, reading the list. To her relief, she found that she had already read over half the books suggested. She then started reading the post-card, since it was only from her aunt, who was in Spain, apparently on the rainy plain, on holiday.

Suddenly all three papers were knocked out of her hand, as she bumped into something very solid, which stood in the middle of the road. Ellie looked up startled, and found that it was the strange man whom she had noticed before. Simultaneously they bent to pick up her post, and cracked their heads sharply together.

'Well, I am sorry, Miss, and no mistake,' said he, rubbing his head.

'It was my fault really,' replied Ellie. 'I was reading, and not looking where I was going either.'

He bent again to pick up the letters. Looking down at him from above, Ellie thought that he reminded her of nothing so much as a white mouse. It wasn't that he had pink eyes and a tail, but it was just the impression given by his face. His nose was very sharp, and his chin receded, while his hair was ash-blond and the eyelashes and brows above the pale grey eyes were almost invisible.

He wiped the electricity bill on the shiny seat of his blue pinstripe trousers, and handed the letters to Ellie. She noticed that he was altogether rather shabby. The cuffs of his maroon sweater were frayed, and a long strand of wool dangled over his right hand. Ellie's fingers itched with the impulse to pull it, and watch the sweater sleeve unravel itself. He wore lopsided brown suede shoes from which the suede had mostly worn away, leaving them as shiny as his trousers' seat.

He smiled at her, showing yellow teeth, and Ellie saw the mouse resemblance growing. It made her want to giggle, because she suddenly had a vivid picture of him in her mind's eye, squeaking and running away on all fours.

'Might I ask if you live in the village, Miss?' he asked, in a disappointingly human voice.

'Yes,' said Ellie, 'I live just here, in the white house with the thatch. I always have. Can I help you? Are you looking for someone? I saw you peering at all the front doors lower down the village.'

The man appeared confused, and rubbed his forehead again.

'No, no, no one in particular,' he said. 'I just came round Tambley way for a stroll. What I *am* interested in is those chrysanths in your front window there.'

Over his shoulder, Ellie saw Mr Kennedy's eldest son

John coming round the bend with their new combine. Angus was pottering about on the other side of the road.

'Gus!' she shouted. 'Gus, come here!'

He ran over to her, and Ellie held him between her ankles until John had passed by, leaning over to smile and wave.

When he had gone, the man looked down at Angus.

'That your dog?' he asked. Ellie felt this to be an unnecessary question, since he so obviously was her dog. She nodded.

'Deaf, is he?' persisted the man. 'You had to holler at him, didn't you?'

'He is a little deaf now,' Ellie admitted, but added

defensively, 'He's getting on though. He's over thirteen.'

'Is he now? Come on, old boy; let's give you a pat.' He chirruped and stretched out his hand.

Angus brushed past him disdainfully, and disappeared through the hedge. He always ignored anyone outside the family.

'Well, those chrysanths I was admiring when I got in your way—could you tell me if they are live ones or imitation?' the man asked.

It was beginning to rain in the wind and Ellie wanted to get away.

'They are imitation. They're made of wood,' she replied, and moved towards the gate.

The man sidled after her. 'Do they make them in the village, then? Or did you get them in Bewley?'

He seemed anxious, and Ellie began to dislike him. She explained quickly about their having bought them from a gipsy at the Bewley cross-roads.

'Long ago then, was it?' the man asked.

'A week ago yesterday,' Ellie answered, and put her hand on the gate.

'A gipsy? Did he have a dog with him?' The man's voice was getting higher in his anxiety to keep her talking.

Ellie thought that soon he might really begin squeaking, and looked at him hopefully to see if he became more mouse-like. He didn't, and she nodded, went in, and shut the gate behind her.

'Wait just a minute, Miss, please,' said the man, and craned over the privet hedge, staring intently at the chrysanthemums.

'I'll buy them.' The words seemed to burst from him. 'I'll give you a good price, if you'll sell them to me.' He put his hand in his pocket. 'For my wife,' he added.

Ellie disliked him even more.

'I'm sorry,' she said coldly, 'but they are definitely not for sale. I really must go now. I've got the sausages with me, and my father will be waiting for his meal.'

As she turned the corner of the house, she saw him still standing there, peering desperately through the sitting-room window.

'Have you been *making* those sausages?' asked Roger, coming out to throw away the potato peelings. 'It's nearly tea-time already.'

Ellie ignored him, and hurried in to beg some raw potato before they were put on the stove.

'Have you seen your father? He's supposed to be mending that banister rail that Roger broke last week,' said Mother.

'No,' replied Ellie. 'He's not in the village.'

Roger came back and Ellie struck an heroic attitude before him.

'When did you last see your father?' she asked him sternly.

'I do not know. My lips are sealed and I am dumb,' replied Roger, hanging his head.

'Well, that's a change,' remarked Daddy, coming in through the back door and brushing rain-drops off his shirt. 'Why didn't anyone tell me it was raining?'

'We lost you, dear,' said Mother, and laid the broken banister rail tenderly in his arms.

'Oh yes. I went out for my hammer, didn't I?' said Daddy.

'An hour ago that was,' said Roger. 'Even before Ellie went out for the sausages.'

'All I did was to see if the hammock was still safe,' explained Daddy, assuming an injured expression. 'I lay down on it to make sure that it was, and found *The Swiss Family Robinson* already there. So then I read a little piece to see if I still remembered it and when I woke up, it was raining.'

He laid the book on the table. Jane walked round him to look in his trouser pockets.

'I'll go and get you the hammer,' she said kindly, 'and I hope that Ellie hasn't forgotten the sausages too.'

'Of course not,' said Ellie. 'I had to wait in the shop, as usual, and then I met Joe with some mail. Here's one from Aunt Nancy for you, Mother, and one from the Electricity Board for you, Daddy. I do hope it's a nice one.'

'It never has been yet,' said Daddy, taking it. 'Hey, who's been chewing this up? Couldn't you gnaw a dog biscuit instead.' He waved the smudged and muddy envelope before her.

'Oh, I didn't do that,' said Ellie. 'The Mouse-man did it.'

'Whoever is that, dear?' asked Mother.

'Have you been drinking?' asked Daddy.

'Where is he?' asked Jane. 'Has he got whiskers?'

'I know,' said Roger, 'he's one of those invisible beings that get blamed for things, like the Borrowers.'

'No, he's not then,' said Ellie, 'he's as real as you are. It's just that he looks like a white mouse, because of his quivery nose and his hair.'

'But where *is* he?' repeated Jane.

'I expect he's on his way home,' said Ellie. 'I followed him up the road from the shop, and bumped into him just outside, because I was reading. I dropped the letters and he picked them up, and rubbed yours on the seat of his trousers, Daddy. It was wet, and his trousers were dirty, so that was that.

'He wanted to buy the wooden chrysanthemums,' she added, 'but I told him they weren't for sale.'

'You're a ninnyhammer,' said Roger, 'we could have made a profit on them and emigrated to Australia.'

'No, I'd rather stay here and keep them,' said Mother. 'I like the climate.'

It rained steadily all afternoon and evening then, and all they could do was play rummy and tiddlywinks.

On Sunday, everyone woke late and irritable, because it was so dark. The rain dripped continuously from the eaves and the apple-trees and the clothes-line, and turned all the flowers inside out and upside down. They splashed off to church in wellington boots and plastic macs and umbrellas, and even the Vicar seemed unable to find much inspiration.

Misery increased all the afternoon, except for Daddy, who retired to the sitting-room to study the political situation, or, as Roger said, to have a nap. Jane wailed because she couldn't find her paint-brushes, and Mother had to make her a temporary one with some of Angus's hair. Roger's temper grew shorter as he grew more nervous at the prospect of Bewley Grammar in the morning, and being a junior again instead of a top boy. He fought with Ellie over the ownership of the one eraser in the house, and Mother had to solve the problem by halving it with a razor-blade.

Ellie couldn't find her hockey-stick or her hockey-boots until half an hour before supper-time and when she did, the boots wouldn't fit her. Altogether, the atmosphere was one of acute depression and apprehension, suitable to the evening before the Black Monday of the return to school.

When at last the three of them were in bed, Angus climbed out of his box where he had discreetly remained, and Daddy stretched his legs over the hearth-rug with a contented sigh.

'It's strange,' he said, 'but by tomorrow morning, they'll be full of enthusiasm.'

4

Black Monday

ROGER WOKE UP still feeling miserable, but as it was only six o'clock, decided that he'd better stay where he was for a while. The sun was shining full on his window-pane, and with every movement that he made, dust danced in the sunbeams. He knew that he'd never go back to sleep, so he reached *Stalky and Co.* down from his book-shelf, and depressed himself still further by reading the chapter about fags and bullies. He gave it up in despair.

Then the black and yellow shirt hanging over his chair reminded him of football. He thought joyfully of playing on a proper pitch, with full teams of boys all the same size. Last winter at the village school, they'd even had to play four girls in, because there were not enough boys. He shuddered at the memory of it. Then there would be swimming, too, and cross-country running, and doing biology with microscopes and everything.

He took down *Stalky* again, and read the chapter about the huts in the furze. This so cheered and strengthened him that he decided to get up quietly and light the fire, but he was surprised to find that it was already a quarter past seven. By the time that he had washed extra well, and decided to throw dignity to the winds and ask Mother to tie his tie for him, it was twenty to eight and Mother had breakfast nearly ready.

'Have you heard Jane stirring yet?' she asked.

Roger sat on the back door-step in the sun to put his shoes on.

'Yes, they were fighting for the tooth-paste a few moments ago,' he replied. 'How long do you think it will take us to bike into Bewley?'

Mother smiled at him, seeing him glance anxiously at the clock.

'Certainly not an hour and a quarter, so don't get worried,' she said. 'Oh, did I forget to tell you? I saw Peter on Friday, and he said that he'll be calling at about twenty past eight.'

'Good. Eggo's coming with us too, if his Dad's kept his promise about a bike.'

'Whoever is Eggo?' asked Mother, putting the tea-pot on the table.

'His name is really Adolph Hudson,' said Roger. 'His father's just moved to that chicken-farm down by the Hall, so we call him Eggo after the hens, or else Addled which is hens and Adolph mixed. Can I begin mine?'

'Yes, you'd better,' said Mother. 'I'll go and see what the girls are up to.'

The door burst open as she spoke, and Jane hopped across the kitchen and out of the back door.

'Where are you hopping off to, Janey?' called Mother. 'Your egg will be stone-cold in a second and a half.'

'She's practising for the pantomime,' explained Ellie, closing the hall door. 'She says she's going to be the leading frog.'

'Pantomime!' said Daddy, opening the hall door again. 'Let's get Christmas over first. Is there anything hot left in the kettle, Mary? Roger's washed his ears to celebrate and it's taken a whole tankful of hot water to do it. Don't they both look smart, though? I feel like a tramp steamer in the yacht basin!'

He went back upstairs to shave, and Jane hopped on to her chair.

At a quarter past eight Roger was trying on his new school cap at different angles, when there was a loud and prolonged jangling of bicycle bells in the road. He decided that the cap on the back of his head made his ears stick out least, and tore round to the garage to get his bike. When he wheeled it round to the front gate he found everyone there to give him a send-off and, as Ellie said, to see what Peter looked like when he hadn't any straws in his hair. Peter was Mr Kennedy's second son; John, the elder, worked full-time on the farm now.

Ellie went round to admire Eggo's new bike and thoughtfully removed two feathers from the back of his coat.

'Thanks very much,' he said. 'I shall have enough to put up with today, without any eggy jokes. This tie is strangling me.'

'John asked me to give you his apologies, Ellie,' said Peter, grinning.

'Whatever for?' she asked.

'Oh, for interrupting your conversation with the boy-friend on Saturday morning when he was on the combine. He said that he looked a very interesting character!'

Ellie laughed. 'He looked just like a human mouse, and he was more horrible than interesting. He wanted to buy those, for some unknown reason.' She pointed through the window to the chrysanthemums.

'It's more usual for gipsy-types to be selling them, isn't

it?' said Peter. 'Are you ready, Roger? I suppose we ought
to be off.'

The three of them rode away, with the stiff and shiny
satchels bumping on their backs.

'They look like three twins now,' said Jane, waving her
bread and butter enthusiastically in farewell.

'You mean triplets, you know,' said Ellie, removing a
piece of Jane's bread from her hair. 'Goodness, here's the
Riddington bus already. Keep it for me, Daddy, please.'

She shot into the kitchen to grab her beret and her
satchel and to beg for 'a little something' for break-time.

'You'll be as fat as Pooh soon,' said Jane severely.

Daddy waved the bus off, then came in for a last cup of
tea.

'It makes me feel young again, to be waved at by thirty
young ladies,' he said. 'I see they've given them the luxury-
tour coach again though. It grieves me to think of us poor
old business men having to bump into Bewley in that
hundred-year-old veteran bus that they only keep out of
sentiment, while they go hushing along in that lovely
machine.'

'Well, they are the rising generation and so they must
be cherished,' said Mother.

Jane went off last of all, and Mother and Angus stood
outside to watch her skipping down the main street to the
village school. Then they went back to the house, Mother
to do an enormous amount of holiday washing, and Angus
to sit out in the garden, well away from the splashes.

Promptly at two minutes past four the usual stream of
cycles surged out of the main gates of the Bewley Boys'
Grammar School. They were followed by school buses and

boys running or dawdling or fighting surreptitiously among themselves.

Peter, Roger and Eggo turned right, instead of left to Tambley, and went down into Bewley looking for extra strong peppermints with which to fortify themselves. They rode back to the cross-roads in a warm silence, and turned down the Tambley road.

'Well,' said Peter, 'that was all right, wasn't it? Super gym, and I'm looking forward to some proper football too. No more dame-school stuff for us now.'

'Oh, ar,' said Eggo in agreement. He pedalled backwards down the slope to the bridge over the River Ridding, and his chain came off.

'It's because it's new,' said Roger, fitting it back on. 'It's not bedded in yet.'

Eggo squatted to watch him. 'Meant to tell you before,' he said, 'but we've had too much to think about. Dad had to take the police all over the farm again this Saturday.'

'Were they probing about with rods then, looking for rotten bodies?' asked Peter. 'Where are they starting digging?'

Eggo laughed, and held his nose. 'If they dig the whole farm, they'll find nothing worse than a heap of mouldy feathers down near the hen-houses. You don't need to be digging to find them, anyway. You can smell them a mile off. They didn't touch anything. The inspector from Riddington was with them this time, and he said he just wanted to see the lie of the land.'

Roger thought for a moment. 'The break-in will be just a fortnight ago on this Thursday, won't it? I should think that Mr Maitland's about given up hope,' he said.

'Dad told me that Inspector Charles thinks that the man's

been lying fast somewhere, waiting for the opportunity to pass the silver to a fence. They haven't traced any of it yet. I asked the Inspector if he'd be likely to melt it down, but he said there was no fear of that in this case. What made Mr Maitland's silver valuable was the engraving.'

The chain finally slipped back and Roger gave it a small kick to make sure. They pedalled fast down the hill to the bridge to give themselves a good run up the hill into Tambley. Just before the village, Eggo left them to turn up the lane leading to Mr Maitland's estate, which was Highcomb Hall, the woods and three cottages, and to Mr Hudson's chicken-farm on the left before the Hall gates.

Kennedy's farm was on the Tambley slope of Highcomb Hill, and Peter left Roger in the village and bumped away up the farm road among the pot-holes.

Roger very nearly ran Jane over then, because she jumped straight out of the shop in front of him, to beg a ride up on his cross-bar.

Mother looked up from cutting bread and smiled at them. Angus licked Roger on his leg, which was his usual greeting.

'Well, do you think you're going to enjoy it, dear?' asked Mother. 'Were you there in plenty of time?'

'Yes, heaps. We're going at half past eight tomorrow,' said Roger. 'I feel as though I've been there a year already, because there are quite a few boys that I know. David Fletcher is head prefect this term, but he even stopped and spoke to me. He was at Miss Pilgrim's for a year when I first started. Is there anything to eat?'

'In just one moment,' replied Mother. 'Will you give Ellie a call for me? She's upstairs somewhere, I think. I'm rather late today, because two strange policemen and P.C.

Pilgrim came an hour ago, just when I wanted to be iron-ing.'

Roger bellowed 'Tea' up Ellie's back stairs. 'What were the policemen doing then?' he asked. 'Was Inspector Charles one of them? He's just been put on the case, so Eggo told me, and he was at their farm on Saturday. I suppose it was about the Hall's silver, was it? It's a pity that Timothy couldn't have solved it by himself; they might have made him a sergeant. Still, I suppose he'll enjoy having someone to talk to about it, and to go round the village with.'

'Yes, I think it was an Inspector Charles, but they were only checking up to make sure that no one had seen any strangers in the village that evening,' said Mother, butter-ing pikelets at a great rate. 'You mustn't call Constable Pilgrim Timothy when he's on duty, though, Roger. It's rather disrespectful. I know he's a great friend of yours, but he is the village policeman after all, and Jane will only do it too if she hears you.'

Ellie came into the kitchen just as Daddy opened the back door, and saw the pikelets.

'Do you know,' he said, hanging his coat up in a frenzy and missing the hook, 'I had a positive compulsion to finish at four-thirty and catch the early bus. Now I realize that it was a pikelet calling me home.'

'What sort of a voice does a pikelet have, then, Daddy?' inquired Jane seriously, licking butter out of the holes.

'It has a warm, greasy voice, that trickles in one ear and out of the other,' explained Daddy, butter running down his chin.

'A pikelet must be a greasy character altogether,' said Roger.

It was a rather noisy evening, and everyone seemed to be talking at once. Roger wanted to describe his new school, and Ellie and Jane simultaneously brought everyone up to date with all the Riddington and village school gossip.

Quite a lot of this seemed to have been about the burglary at Highcomb Hall.

'It's very odd,' said Ellie, 'but quite a few girls seem to have seen a suspicious-looking man loitering round in Tambley that evening. All of them seem to be different men though!'

'Perhaps it was a gang, then,' suggested Roger. 'Dozens of evil men with padded shoulders, crêpe soles, greasy neck-ties and scarred faces, all converging on Castle Tambley!'

'Goodness, the Hall silver isn't *so* valuable,' said Daddy. 'I should think it is much more likely that these crowds of suspicious-looking characters turn out to be gate-posts, or cows looking over fences, or ivy blowing on a wall, or some such.'

Jane's eyes had been growing wider throughout this discussion, so that Mother suggested a game of tiddlywinks before she went to bed, to take her mind off Roger's 'dozens of evil men'.

This seemed to make even more noise, however, and Daddy expressed the pious hope that their teachers would soon feel themselves capable of beginning homework.

5

The Mouse Squeaks

ROGER SEEMED TO have so much to think about that his mind simply refused to shut itself off, and be quiet, and go to sleep. The more he worried about not going to sleep, and consequently being late in the morning, the more wide-awake he became and the more lumpy the mattress. He found his torch and looked at the clock in desperation. It was already half past twelve.

He decided to play a small trick on himself, which had worked once or twice before. He cautiously sat up in bed, and reached up to his book-shelf to find his *Observer's Book of Birds*. Then he sat straight and still and convinced himself that he had to learn five pages of birds before the morning. He then retreated backwards down the bed, propped the book against the pillow, and switched on his torch. He knew from past experience that when his brain was required to concentrate and do some solid work, it immediately became limp and exhausted and insisted on going to sleep.

But after ten minutes his mind wandered again, moving from the markings and habits of the moor-hen in English ponds to Scott's small tent alone in the bitter wastes of the Antarctic. His bed reminded him of a tent in miniature, held up over the hump of his back, lit by the soft glow of his torch, warm inside yet with the cold night air creeping in at the top. He shuffled farther down the bed, so that the crack at the top closed, and no air came in at all.

He was trying to memorize the plumage of the crested grebe, and admittedly becoming very drowsy, when he suddenly had the feeling that some horrible and unknown creature was creeping up to sit on the top of his bed and so suffocate him, as if he were a miner trapped in a coal-seam. He shot up the bed into the air, his neck and back prickling with fright, and found his bedroom as always, cold and quiet, with a little moonlight coming through the curtains. His jacket hung dark against the white paint of the door, and the familiar wardrobe stood solid and comforting in the corner. He lay still, with his ears stretched, and his heart thudding against his ribs and the bed-clothes.

Suddenly Roger raised his head a little from the pillow and opened his eyes wide, staring into the darkness, listening. It had been a mouse, squeaking somewhere. He was sure that he had heard it. It came again, and he smiled to himself, thinking how cross Mother would be if it were in his bedroom, although he couldn't think why it should be. He never had any food upstairs.

He was quite wide-awake now, and lay listening for the little sound to come again. It did, and Roger was puzzled. He was certain that it wasn't in his bedroom. It seemed to come from outside, in the garden, yet surely he'd never hear a mouse so far away. The squeak wasn't quite mouse-like either, now that he heard it clearly again. It was too harsh and high a note. He wondered if it was perhaps a baby owl, sitting on the telegraph wires.

Roger's bedroom was on the front of the house, below Ellie's and above the front room. Only a few feet of garden separated the house from the road, and the telegraph wires were immediately opposite his window.

The squeak came again, and was followed by a soft thud. Roger pushed the book and the torch under the pillow, and quietly pulled back the bed-clothes. He thought now that a hedgehog, or perhaps even an owl, had been hit by a passing car and thrown on to the side of the road.

He walked softly over to the window and slowly drew the curtain to one side. The village stood grey in the moon-light and the trees were absolutely still. It certainly hadn't been one tree branch rubbing against another. Roger looked hard, and could see nothing in the road either. He stood close to the glass, peering down at their privet-hedge, and the squeak came once again. It was short, harsh, and it set his teeth on edge, and this time it was followed by a sigh.

Roger craned forward and stared down at the house-front. The shadows moved. A man stepped a pace back from the sitting-room window, and wiped his hands on his handkerchief. Roger moved back into his room, and gently let the curtain fall.

He felt hot with excitement. He realized that the squeaks were made by the catch on the window, as the man below tried to force it back. He stood in the dark room, and wondered what to do.

His father was notoriously difficult to wake, and anyway always snorted and grunted loudly in the process. The man could be a hundred yards away before either of his parents was fully awake and out of bed. Roger made up his mind to manage this himself, to begin with.

He knew that the sitting-room door was ajar. He could creep downstairs quietly and so have a good view of the man's face at the window. The moon was clear enough.

Then he could ring the dinner bell that his mother kept on the hall table to call them in from the orchard end, and rush out in pursuit of the man, with Angus. He had no doubt that his father would soon catch them up, as he was a good runner still. If only he, Roger, could keep the man in sight.

He moved softly to his bedroom door, and opened it by pulling on his jacket. He dared not touch the knob, as it was an old brass one and very loose and rattly. He crept slowly along the landing to the stair-head, feeling his warm feet stick to the polished floor. He cautiously shifted his weight from the landing floor to the top stair. That was an awkward moment, because if you moved too suddenly, a dreadful creak ran down the full length of the staircase. He stood still, and seemed to hear the whole house breathing round him.

The squeak sounded again, very faintly, this time through the open door of the sitting-room below him. It's a good thing, thought Roger to himself, that Angus is old now and fairly deaf. He knew the disposition of every plank on the stairs, and trod gently down them, putting his feet on the side of each step where from long experience he knew that they creaked less.

He was only six steps from the hall and the open door to the sitting-room, when his pyjama buttons rapped sharply against the banister rail. Roger stood as though frozen, but heard Angus climb out of his box, and walk over the kitchen floor to the hall door, his paws pattering on the tiles. He sniffed loudly under the crack of the door, and began to growl softly, just to himself. Roger held his breath.

From the sitting-room came a last agonized squeak, and a sharp crack. Angus gave one short suspicious bark, and Roger heard the man swear softly. He leapt down the remaining stairs and burst into the sitting-room as Angus began to bark angrily and in earnest.

There was no sign of the man at all, only the gate swinging silently back on its hinges, and a round hole cut in the top window-pane, nearest the catch. Roger stared at it stupidly, and through the hole the moon stared back at him.

He ran to the kitchen, and fell over Angus as soon as he opened the door. There was no need now to ring the dinner bell to wake the house!

Daddy came down the stairs three at a time, disguised as a raging fury, or a stern Victorian parent. The effect was rather spoilt when he tripped over Angus and his dressing-gown cord simultaneously, and had to swing on the kitchen door to save himself. Roger, relieved from the tension of the last few minutes, lay happily on the floor and became convulsed with laughter. Daddy switched on the light and stared down at him incredulously.

'What in the whole wide world do you think you're doing, boy?' he demanded. 'Are you mad, or drunk, or both? Why are you lying on the floor laughing at past one o'clock in the morning?'

Roger had no breath left to speak with, and anyway had to fight off Angus, who was butting and licking his face in consternation.

Ellie was next down, and gazed silently at Roger, thinking that he had tripped on his way down to forage in the pantry, and not liking to see him in trouble. Mother firmly put Jane down in bed again, and waited to see her go straight back to sleep. Then she came downstairs, stepped over Roger in a matter-of-fact way, and put the kettle on.

'Now come and sit down sensibly, all of you,' she said, switching on the electric fire. 'You all look much too wide-awake to go back to sleep straight away, so we may as well sort things out here and now. What are you doing down here, Roger?'

The whole story was soon told. Daddy's face relaxed, and he warmed his hands round his tea-cup.

'So you didn't see the man at all?' he asked. 'Had he moved the catch back?'

Roger hadn't noticed, and they trooped into the front room, to examine the hole more closely.

'But it's perfect!' exclaimed Ellie, gently and gingerly running her finger along the cut edge. 'It's almost as if he had done it with a knife.'

'I expect he did it with a diamond cutter,' said Daddy, and peered through the window. 'You can see the round of glass lying on the top of the hedge, just by the gate-post. It's reflecting the moon.'

'Of course,' said Roger. 'That explains the squeaks, doesn't it? It wasn't nearly enough noise to wake any of us, or even Angus, really. It was only because I was awake anyway that I heard him at all. If Gus hadn't woken up and interfered, we might have had him by now.'

'I think on the whole that I'm glad he did,' said Mother.

Daddy nodded in agreement. 'If you had chased after him, he'd probably have lain in wait behind the nearest tree, and nobbled you as you went by. Then we should have been even worse off.'

They went back to the kitchen to finish their tea. Angus squeezed between Ellie's feet and the table-leg, and inched himself between her and the fire. She scratched the top of his head with her slipper.

'He's a good old dog and was only doing his best,' she said. 'Anyway, he can't be as deaf as we thought.'

'Ha!' exclaimed Daddy. 'There's none so deaf as those that won't hear. He can hear well enough when it suits him to.'

'That horrid man was rude about him being deaf,' Ellie said, and her face lit up. 'That's who it was. That's who it was for sure. I knew he'd squeak if I waited long enough, and now he has!'

'If you mean your Mouse-man,' said Mother, 'what would he go to all this trouble to get in for? The house doesn't look exactly prosperous.'

'I know,' said Ellie. 'I know why. He wanted the wooden chrysanthemums for his wife.'

Roger was reduced to rolling on the floor again, shaking with laughter.

'No, Ellie dear,' said Daddy, smiling, 'I can't see any man going to the trouble of laboriously cutting a hole in our window in the middle of the night, just because his wife is nagging him to get her some chrysanthemums. If he wanted them so badly, he could have waited till we were out, heaved a brick through it, and been away before anyone found where the crash came from.'

'What a pity,' said Ellie. 'The squeaking fitted in with him so nicely.'

Mother collected the cups and looked at the clock. 'Well, it's a quarter past one and you can't speculate about your Mouse-man any more tonight, or rather this morning. What are you going to do about reporting it, John? Now, or after breakfast? Do you think he'll come back, for any odd reason?'

'Oh, no,' said Daddy. 'I don't see why he should do that. To keep you from fidgeting about it, though, I'll lock the sitting-room door, and leave the kitchen door into the hall open, so that Angus will be able to hear anything that happens.'

'What about the police, then?' said Mother. 'After breakfast?'

'Yes, Timothy Pilgrim won't relish being woken at this

early hour. I don't suppose he will object, as long as we don't touch anything before he arrives.' Daddy yawned and stretched hugely, knocking against the electric light and sending it swinging in wild circles.

'It makes me feel sea-sick when it does that,' said Ellie, standing on tiptoe to steady it. 'Have we got to go to bed again, now?'

'Yes, of course, and at once,' replied Mother. 'What do you think? You can't want breakfast already.'

'I do,' replied Roger, making his stomach gurgle in a rude way. 'It would save a lot of time getting up, if we didn't go to bed. I don't feel at all sleepy.'

Nevertheless, he followed the other three upstairs and, when he saw Mother straightening his bed, suddenly could hardly keep his eyes open. He slid straight down between the sheets, still faintly warm, and knocked the torch from under his pillow. Mother picked it up, and set it on its end on the mantelpiece, like a small lighthouse.

Roger quivered with laughter again, as he remembered something.

'Do you know what is the funniest thing about the whole affair?' he said. 'The back door was open all the time.'

6

Pilgrim's Progress

THE LEYLANDS WERE not on the telephone. Daddy insisted that he would have to work too much overtime if they were, and said that he liked to have the feeling that his boss could not get in touch with him in an emergency.

Consequently, when Peter and Eggo rang their bicycle bells outside at half past eight the next morning, the whole family, with the exception of Mother, ambled round the house corner looking extremely drowsy. Mr Leyland was carrying three envelopes; Ellie was carrying a duster to lay over the round of glass still lying on the hedge; Jane was carrying Angus, and Roger was carrying a slice of bread and dripping. He hadn't his tie or his cap on.

Peter looked at his watch to make sure that it was half past eight, and not half past seven. Eggo pushed a polite smile on to his face, instead of an astonished stare.

'Oh,' said Peter. 'Have you decided that you don't like Bewley already, Roger? Or have you got measles?'

Roger merely shook his head in reply and turned to point dramatically with his free hand to the hole in the window, and with the slice of bread and dripping to the missing piece of glass lying on the hedge.

' 'Strewth, who managed to do that?' asked Eggo, putting out his hand to pick up the glass for a closer look.

Roger intercepted the hand and gave it back over the

hedge, then took the duster from Ellie and laid it over the glass with a flourish.

'You'll have Timothy Pilgrim after you if you go greasing up his lovely finger-prints,' he said, and told what had happened for the second time.

The two of them were properly impressed, and on principle very envious that Roger had a good excuse for getting off a morning's school. In actual fact, it would be a handicap rather than an advantage as Roger would miss the giving out of lesson and homework timetables, locker numbers, and various other new-school routines, and have to do some copying up in his own time.

'Now I wonder if you will do me a favour,' said Daddy, looking at his watch. 'Will you have time? It is really three favours, anyway.'

He handed the three envelopes over the gate to Peter.

'One of these is for your form master, to excuse Roger from school until Constable Pilgrim has finished asking him questions. The second is for my own boss, doing the same. It's the office block on the corner of Wellington Street, about two minutes down from the school gates, and you need only hand it in to the porter. The third one is for Mr Catlin whose workshop is nearly opposite to the school itself, fortunately. The women in this house don't feel safe, being left with a handy hole in the window. They want Mr Catlin to come and put a new pane in before tonight. Can you manage that, do you think?'

They said that they thought they could, and rode away.

Ellie's bus arrived five minutes later, and Jane was sent five minutes early to school to take a note into P.C. Pilgrim, who was the brother of the village school-mistress.

When she reached the square red-brick police-house, the

newest one in the village, she found that she didn't have to go in at all. P.C. Pilgrim was standing on a kitchen stool, fixing a poster about a police dance at Bewley up on the notice-board by the front gate.

He was humming busily to himself and didn't notice Jane until she pulled at his coat and said, 'Hello, Timothy.'

He peered down at her under his elbow while he struggled with an insubordinate drawing-pin.

'Timothy, is it?' he said. 'And who told you that my name is Timothy, then? Maybe it's Ernest or Arthur or Joseph or Frank. Timothy isn't a proper sounding name for a policeman, now is it?'

'No,' said Jane. 'Not really. But you must have once been a little boy, and your mother probably didn't know that you would turn into a policeman. Perhaps you had curly hair and looked like a Timothy then.'

'Perhaps I did,' he agreed, and stepped down from the stool. 'On your way to school, are you, Janey? You'd better be skipping along, before my sister wonders where you are. She might think that you're not coming today and put you a little *a* in the register.'

He picked up his stool, and opened the gate.

'Well,' said Jane, 'I nearly forgot after all. I've got a letter for you from Daddy. I'd better wait and see if you want to answer it.'

She took the envelope carefully from her pocket and gave it to him, then sat on the stool whilst he read it and practised reading herself on the police-dance poster.

'This will be a little excitement for Tambley,' he said. 'And a good thing that Roger did go mouse-hunting in the middle of the night.'

'Yes,' said Jane. 'But I only went back to sleep. I was in bed the whole time.'

'The best place for you, that was,' said Constable Pilgrim picking up the stool again, and putting the letter in his pocket. 'And now the best place for you is with my Elizabeth, so just you run along there sharpish. I can hear them singing the hymn without you. I'll be up to see your Dad straight away.'

'All right then,' said Jane. 'Good-bye.'

'Good-bye,' he said. 'And don't let your mother hear you calling me Timothy, else she'll be after me.'

'No, I won't do,' promised Jane, and trotted down towards the school.

Constable Pilgrim went into the house looking for his helmet to make him more official, and then walked quickly up the hill to the Leylands'. As he turned the corner by the back door, he trod heavily on Angus's tail as he lay stretched out in a patch of thin sunlight, and stooped hurriedly to make apology for it. Angus licked his hand, wagging his tail briefly in polite acceptance, and went with him to the back door.

Roger opened the door as they got to it, and found Constable Pilgrim knocking on the air.

'I'm sorry,' he said, and closed it again.

This time Constable Pilgrim knocked on it with both fists, beating a small tattoo, and saying, 'Let me in. Open in the name of the law.'

Roger opened it again. 'I ain't done nothin',' he said. 'And if I had you couldn't prove it.'

'Ha,' said Timothy. 'You underestimate me, Master Roger. My record is a brilliant one, and by rights I should be a sergeant, or even an inspector.'

Roger laughed, and knocked on the wall to let Daddy know that he was here, because he was looking for a screw-driver that he had lost in the garage. Mother came downstairs and smiled at P.C. Pilgrim.

'I'll put the kettle on,' she said. 'You'd like a cup of tea, wouldn't you?'

'Yes, please,' said Daddy, coming in at the back door. 'Is your pencil sharp, Timothy?'

'Always is, Mr Leyland,' said Constable Pilgrim. 'Always ready.'

'You must know that Timothy's our scout-master, Pa,' said Roger. 'Be prepared—remember?'

'Of course I remember,' said Daddy. 'I can follow a trail with the best of you and light a fire with half a match, providing it's the right half, of course.'

Mother laughed. 'But I've told you, Roger,' she said, 'that you mustn't call Constable Pilgrim Timothy when he's on duty. He has a position to keep up in the village.'

Timothy put his helmet on and looked grim. Then he took it off again and sat down at the kitchen table with his note-book.

Roger told him with speed and great inaccuracy exactly what might have happened in the night, then they all had a cup of tea. Afterwards Roger told the story again, this time at a writing speed and with no embellishments. He signed the statement, and Timothy put the note-book away. He drew out a small tin from his pocket, and shook it gently.

'Good,' he said, when it rattled. 'I thought maybe Elizabeth had borrowed it again. She's always losing her own.'

He twisted off the lid, and took out a tape-measure.

'Do you mind if I measure up the hole now, Mrs Leyland?' he asked.

'Of course not,' replied Mother.

They followed him into the sitting-room and Roger held the end of the tape-measure for him. He measured the length of the window-pane and the breadth. He measured the distance of the hole from the catch, the top, and both sides of the window. He measured the height of the window-sill from the ground. He measured the diameter of the hole. He turned round.

'Mrs Leyland . . .' he began

'I know,' said Roger. 'He wants to take out the whole window-frame! There might be dozens of clues on it. Shall I go and fetch the chisel for you, to knock away the putty?'

Constable Pilgrim laughed and rolled up the tape-measure. 'Now then,' he said. 'Nothing like that at all. I was wondering if you could lend me the duster that's over the piece of glass on the hedge, Mrs Leyland? Just to wrap it in while I take it down to the house.'

'Yes, of course,' said Mother.

He sat at the table again to copy the measurements neatly into his note-book.

'Are you blinding them with science?' asked Daddy.

'Not exactly,' he replied. 'But it does help to fill out the report, and they always seem to like a few figures. I don't think that a photograph of a hole would help in this case, so that would seem to be all for now. I'll let you know, of course, if anything turns up, but I don't suppose that anyone will have seen the man at that time of night.'

He put the tape-measure back in its tin, and the note-book back in its pocket, collected the round of glass from the hedge, and went away down the hill to the village.

Roger got to Bewley only in time for half a lesson before dinner. He found himself the centre of interest for a short time, and various suggestions were made as to how he should have gone about catching the burglar.

The most popular of these was put forward by Simon Wilkins, a small spectacled boy with a reedy voice and legs like a sparrow. He spent three-quarters of his waking life dreaming of improbable adventures which were liberally sprinkled with escaped lions, spies, and space-ships, and in which he appeared always as tall, handsome, muscular, and courageous.

'You should have put more thought into it, Leyland,' he said. 'The best way to have nailed him would have been to let yourself fall from your bedroom window on to his head.'

By four o'clock everyone, including Roger, had for-gotten the whole affair. The three of them rode home to Castle Tambley lustily singing the unprinted and unprint-able words to the school song that had been handed down through generations of boys, and had that afternoon been revealed to them.

When Roger wheeled his bicycle through the gate, he found Jane waiting there for Mr Catlin.

'Mother wants some butter fetched from the shop,' she informed him. 'I'm waiting for Mr Catlin and Ellie's got a choir practice, so you have to go.'

'Well, let me get my breath!' said Roger indignantly. 'I've had a hard day. Why can't you go?'

'Putty,' replied Jane, and breathed on her hand in readi-ness.

'Oh, blow you!' said Roger. 'They're bound to keep me talking about last night and it'll take me one and a half hours.'

He went out of the gate with Angus and the butter money as Mr Catlin came in with his bag and a pane of glass wrapped in sacking.

Jane seized on him at once and was busy prising off the lid of his putty tin while he went in to have a word with Mother. She loved to warm putty and soften it and fashion it into various shapes—animals, and little pots, and flowers. It had to be kept warm and moist though, or it suddenly disintegrated into crumbs. Mr Catlin came back and gave her a good lump of it. Jane squatted on the grass beside him, and Mr Catlin whistled through his teeth as he worked, chipping the old dry putty from the edge of the cut pane.

It was twenty minutes before Roger came back, full of indignation.

'They wanted to hear all about it, as usual,' he said. 'And who told Betty that the man had a gun, anyway? And who told Miss Pilgrim that all we had in the house was twelve and eightpence and a button in the housekeeping purse? The whole village will think we're paupers!'

Jane by now had forgotten what she had said to anybody, and continued to roll the putty into a sausage between her palms. She offered it to Roger to sniff. Angus had a sniff, too, and hurried off to the back door, sneezing.

Mother came round, then, to say that tea was ready and would Mr Catlin like a cup? Jane took her putty with her and finally made it into a D and left it beside Daddy's plate, where it made an oily mark on the tablecloth.

7

Curly-coated Retriever

ANGUS WAS LYING asleep on his side before the fire, and all his paws were twitching. In his dream he began to run up Highcomb Hill after a little grey rabbit and his legs ran on air in his sleep. He yipped and whined in his throat, and still the dream rabbit ran always just ahead. Ellie bent and rubbed his ears, and called him back from the chase up the hill-side to the after-tea time in the kitchen. He peered up at her from one sleepy eye, and thumped his tail twice on the hearth-rug, then went quietly back to sleep, dreamless and rabbitless.

It was Saturday again, and the first week of the autumn term over. The garden outside was dusky enough to make the kitchen feel extra warm and peaceful. Ellie wondered whether to draw the curtains across, to make it definitely evening instead of what was really late afternoon, but decided against it. She liked to watch the sky fading through the branches of the apple-trees, and the outline of Highcomb Hill humping itself up darkly against the night clouds.

Jane was painting at the kitchen table. She always sat on one foot when she was concentrating, letting the other dangle over the chair edge. When one foot went to sleep, she changed it over and sat on the other one. She had half finished the picture and the waterpot needed changing; the water was a thick dark green, with swirls and patches of yellow and red-brown in it. Ellie sat watching her, because she had her maths homework in her lap and was trying to put it off for as long as she could.

Jane's tongue was sticking out of the corner of her mouth, and her nose was only two inches away from the page. She frowned at the dirty water and, after peeping sideways to see if Mother was occupied, sucked the brush clean herself and changed to another colour. After a few minutes Ellie caught her eye, and grinned. Jane opened her mouth wide, and stuck her tongue out for Ellie to see it patterned with bright red and dark blue splodges. Then she shut one eye, and squinted hard down her nose to see it for herself. Ellie changed the water for her.

She could hear Daddy banging away in the garage. He still hadn't finished the ironing-board, and Mother was having to use the table. She sighed now and shook her head over Ellie's school blouse.

'It's not a bit of use,' she said, pushing back her hair. 'My mother never ironed on anything else but the table, and yet she managed all the millions of tucks in my blouses perfectly. I wish she were here now, dear soul, to do the gathers in your blouse, Ellie.'

The bangings in the garage changed to tappings, as Daddy went round the nails, making sure that they were all flush with the wood. He had been fixing a new sheet on the top of the board, because Mother had left the iron sitting on the old one while she went out to the butcher's van. Ellie went round to see how he was getting on, and Angus followed her through the back door.

There was an electric light at one end of the garage, where Daddy had his work bench by the window. Ellie put it on now because it seemed dark to her, coming in from the kitchen. Daddy blinked at her and stretched, and she noticed the sawdust rocking gently in the spiders' webs that festooned the light-bulb.

'Have you finished yet?' she asked. 'Because poor Mother's getting desperate, trying to iron on the table.'

'Come and run your fingers over these nail-heads for me,' he said. 'See if you think they are smooth enough. I shall be in terrible trouble if they catch in anything.'

Ellie put her hand under the board and felt.

'Oh, yes, that'll be all right,' she said, and patted the clean top. 'You've got the sheet good and smooth, haven't you? It's as tight as a drumskin.'

Daddy folded the ironing-board flat, and leant it up

against the bench while he put the nails back in their proper tobacco tin.

'Now I'm ready for my tea,' he remarked, dusting his hands on his trousers' seat.

'But you had it,' said Ellie. 'Half an hour ago you had it. You had a brown egg and a white egg, and you had about half the dough-loaf and Roger had the other half and I hardly got any.'

Daddy appeared surprised and thought hard for a moment.

'Hmn,' he said, 'I do remember having a little something, now that you mention it. Well, is it supper-time yet?'

Ellie laughed and opened the door. A crowd of yellow leaves danced in on the wind and spiralled down to the bottom of the garage.

'I know who Roger takes after,' she said. 'There's nothing to choose between you, for greed!'

Daddy charged her with the ironing-board, and ran her into the kitchen. Then he had to go back to put the garage light off. He made Mother pay him for the ironing-board with a buttered scone and cheese and a bottle of beer. Jane had never tasted beer yet, and insisted on having a wine-glass full. When she got it, she found she didn't like it, and poured it into Angus's water-bowl when no one was looking.

Ellie could think of no further excuse now for not beginning her maths, and when she finally started she found that she could do it perfectly easily. She finished it in twenty minutes, after having wasted over an hour in thinking about beginning.

Roger was at Hudson's farm with Peter. They were

making a boat, a cross between a punt and a rowing boat, to keep on the River Ridding below Tambley. Mr Hudson was supervising the work in what had been the cowshed, where the chicken-feed was now stored. It was beginning to be too dark to see properly inside.

'Shall I fetch a lamp in for you boys?' asked Mr Hudson. 'Or have you had enough boat-building for one day?'

'Well, I think I have,' said Peter, who had just hammered the end of his thumb into a plank with great enthusiasm, thinking it was a nail. 'And John's making an extraordinary wireless out of two old ones, so I'm wondering how he's getting on.'

They moved through loose feathers and the smell of hens to the farm gate, where they had left their bikes.

'What about tomorrow, then?' asked Eggo. 'Will you be able to get away?'

They agreed on two o'clock, and Peter and Roger rode together down the estate lane to Tambley. They parted in the village, and Roger remembered that now he had homework, as well as Ellie. He rode fast up the hill past the church because in P.C. Pilgrim's eyes it was lighting-up time, and in Roger's it wasn't nearly.

Consequently he surprised the man squatting on the grass verge outside their house. Angus was sitting just inside the open gate, waiting for Roger, and the man was talking to him and holding out a toffee in a tempting way. Angus ignored both him and the toffee, and he shuffled nearer. Roger came up silently in the twilight and dismounted.

'If that's a toffee you've got there, he'll not touch it,' he said, and looked at the man curiously.

Angus got up, wagging his tail, and trotted over to lick

Roger's leg. The man scrambled hurriedly to his feet, and stood rather foolishly, still holding the toffee.

'Good evening to you,' he said. 'I hope you don't mind me having a chat to your little dog. I'd this old toffee in my pocket and thought he might like to have it. I'm fond of dogs; always have been.'

It sounded sensible enough, and yet Roger couldn't quite believe it. The man seemed nervous and ill at ease, shifting his feet as he spoke, and not looking Roger in the face. Besides this, Roger had a feeling at the back of his mind that he had seen him before, and yet couldn't be certain where, or indeed if he even had.

He patted Angus and smiled at the man.

'No, I'm afraid toffee is no use to him. The only sweets he'll eat are chocolates, and he doesn't get much chance of those. They give them bad teeth, you know, and worms too I think. Have you a dog yourself?'

Roger wanted to keep the man talking for some time longer, while he dipped for the remembrance of that face. He felt that he would remember it soon and that he ought to, because it was not an ordinary face at all.

The man looked down at Angus, who was standing small and pale in the dusk by Roger's bicycle.

'Yes, I've always a dog of sorts,' he replied. 'Big dogs, mostly. What you might call working dogs. I've a curly-coated retriever just now—I don't expect you'll have ever seen one. Gone out of fashion, it seems.'

'Well, that's a coincidence,' said Roger, surprised. 'I'd never even heard of them until a fortnight ago. We saw one, then, over towards Bewley with a gipsy. He was selling wooden chrysanthemums—the gipsy I mean, not the dog.'

He smiled at the man, but he looked back at him unsmiling, and said nothing. Suddenly he turned, muttering 'Good night,' and walked swiftly away into the twilight and tree-shadows, going towards the village. Roger gazed after him, puzzled, and then wheeled his bicycle round to the garage.

Mother had moved Jane from the table, with some difficulty, and was now laying the supper. Roger sniffed happily as he closed the back door.

'Macaroni cheese,' he said.

'Yes,' said Ellie. 'We knew that would fetch you up from Hudson's. Could you even smell it among the hen-houses, then?'

She picked two speckled feathers from his hair, and dropped them into the fire, where they sizzled once and then melted away. Angus walked over to his water-bowl for a drink. He sniffed loudly, and in disgust, and turned away to stand in his bed and sulk.

'What's the matter with Gus?' asked Ellie. 'He's annoyed about something.'

Mother glanced down at his water as she passed to the pantry, and went back to pick it up.

'Aren't you going to finish your beer, John?' she asked innocently.

Daddy tilted the bottle, and peered at the bottom.

'There isn't a speck left,' he said. 'I have done.'

'No,' said Mother. 'The dog's dish is full of it. Give me your glass.'

Daddy pointed at Jane accusingly, and got up to put away his beer bottle and wash Angus's dish out.

'You're a wicked infant altogether,' he said. 'Trying to corrupt the dog when he's led a good and blameless life for thirteen long years.'

Everyone laughed, because Angus looked so martyred, and Jane put down clean water by him and apologized.

They started supper, and Ellie needed cold water too then, because macaroni cheese always has hidden and unexpected pieces of hotness in it.

Roger described the slow progress that they had made on the boat, and then mentioned the strange man whom he had surprised outside the house, talking to Angus.

'He streaked off down the road without a word when I mentioned that gipsy's curly-coated retriever,' he said, 'and I was trying to remember where I had seen him before. Now I shan't be able to sleep for puzzling about it, and then I shall wake up at about three o'clock in the morning and remember, and forget again before I get up.'

Mother suggested that, in that case, he take some paper and a pencil upstairs with him and write it down. Roger thought this a good idea.

'Perhaps it was the chrysanthemum gipsy himself,' suggested Jane. 'Was he dark and curly, like the dog?'

'No, not a bit,' said Roger. 'He was very fair, and his hair was straight and very close to his head, if you know what I mean. It was so white-looking that it seemed more like the fur of some animal than hair. He was smaller than the gipsy too, small and slim.'

He frowned in concentration, annoyed because he couldn't keep his mind from searching in the corners of his memory.

Ellie was staring at him.

'Did he have a high, thin sort of voice?' she asked.

'Yes, he did,' replied Roger.

'Did he keep on smoothing his hair while he talked, in rather a nervous way?'

'Yes, he did,' said Roger.

'Were his eyes very pale, and did he have a long, sharp nose?'

'Yes, yes—who is he?' asked Roger impatiently.

Ellie looked at him complacently.

'You never have seen him before then,' she said. 'You've only heard me describe him.'

'Well, come on then,' said Roger and Daddy together. 'Who is he?'

Ellie looked from one to the other, and hugged herself with enjoyment.

'The Mouse-man,' she said.

8

Lost: Border Terrier . . .

ELLIE MISSED THE school bus home on Monday because she had to go to the dentist's. She jolted slowly to Tambley on the five o'clock service from Riddington, and felt miserable. Every hundred yards, so it seemed, the ancient bus ground to a standstill to let someone on or off. Then it groaned and shuddered as it drew away again, and Ellie expected each time to see the engine run off in front, leaving the rest of the bus sitting in the road.

The man beside her was grumbling. 'Old devil wants taking off the road. Hasn't hardly got the strength to drag the skin off a rice pudding,' he said.

Ellie silently agreed with him. Two of her fillings were temporary ones, and felt like jagged craters to the tip of her exploring tongue. She had a sore place on her tongue, too, where it had tried to interfere with the drill. Ellie longed for a peppermint to take the taste of dentist away.

Monday was by far the worst day of the week this term, she reflected. Besides being Monday, which was a disadvantage for it to begin with, it now had Maths, Latin, and a double period of Physics to burden it still more. Well, it was over now and tomorrow was a good day, her favourite.

As the bus dipped over the Ridding bridge below Tambley, Ellie saw that a mist was beginning to rise and lie gently over the river meadows. The hedges were already looking thin and wintry, and the leaves drooped tiredly on the trees. She hurried up from the bus stop, thinking of the fire and the tea waiting for her in the kitchen.

When she opened the back door, she found that Mother was alone, and washing up already. Ellie's tea was laid on one end of the long table, together with Daddy's.

Mother turned quickly to see who it was. 'Oh, Ellie,' she said, 'earlier than I thought. Have you seen Jane or Roger in the village?'

'No, what are they doing?' Ellie said, taking her school beret and mac through to the cold hall.

'Looking for Angus,' replied Mother. She turned back to the sink. 'No one's seen him since breakfast-time, and you know that's never happened before.'

Ellie stared blankly into the fire, with a stiff feeling in her stomach. It was true. All his life, Angus had been a homey sort of dog, and had never been away on his own for more than four or five hours.

'Even in his young days when he had his private expeditions, before you can remember, he came home for meal-times,' said Mother, vigorously scrubbing the draining-board.

Ellie sat down and ate her tea quickly. She no longer felt hungry and wanted to be outside, to find Jane and Roger. They came in, however, before she had finished, and Daddy with them. He was trying to cheer Jane up.

'I think I know what's happened,' he said. 'I expect he was sniffing about in someone's garden when he had no right to, and they went out for the day and closed the gate behind them. He'll be sitting on their front-door mat, patiently waiting to be let out.'

Jane looked a little happier and more hopeful.

'But we've been all through Tambley, calling him,' objected Roger.

'I don't suppose you've been up all the farm roads though, have you?' asked Daddy. 'There are three cottages out on Mr Maitland's land too, don't forget. If you two can get your homework done before I've finished my tea, we'll have an hour or two out on the bicycles.'

Jane rebelled at once, and clamoured to go too.

'No,' said Mother very firmly, 'definitely not, Janey. You'll be in bed soon after they go.'

Jane stuck her lip out, and made an immediate and private plan to slip away when no one was looking.

'I've got my eye on you too,' warned Mother, knowing all about it, 'but I'll wake you when they come back, if they do find him.'

Jane knew that she had to be content with this. Ellie and Roger did fractions and French verbs at a tremendous rate, and finished just as Daddy sat down with his pipe by the fire.

'Give me just five minutes to be quiet in,' he said, 'and then we'll be away. I expect my tyres will need pumping up because it's at least six months since I last used the bike. Get your own two out and do that for me, and then I shall be ready.'

Jane ran upstairs to fetch Daddy's old gloves and his wet-gardening trilby, in case the mist turned to rain. She laid these, with his coat, on the table, and ran back into the hall to fetch Ellie's and Roger's things.

'I see that I'm not to be allowed a second over my five minutes,' said Daddy, pretending to be grumpy.

'No you are not,' agreed Jane firmly. 'Think of poor old Gussy, as hungry as can be, and cold too, sitting shut up in someone's nasty garden, waiting to be found.'

The three of them set out in quite a cheerful fashion, having convinced themselves that this was the case. They went in wavering single file up Kennedys' pot-holed farm road to call at the two cottages of their farm workers. Neither of them had seen anything of Angus, and Daddy realized that there was no point in going up to the farm itself, as there was so little likelihood of a strange dog getting quietly shut away there. They went back down to the village.

In half an hour they had called at all the outlying cottages and found nothing. No one there had seen him either.

'That only leaves Mr Maitland's place, then,' said Daddy. 'Do you think that Mr Hudson's Sam would be likely to murder Angus on the spot, if he strayed into the chicken-farm, Roger?'

Mr Hudson kept a large and rather savage Alsatian, which was allowed to roam freely at night, in order to act as a deterrent to both foxes and chicken thieves. Since he had bought it, six months ago, Mr Hudson had been troubled by neither and was very pleased with the result of his experiment.

'Oh, no,' replied Roger. 'Sam's supposed to be trained not to kill, but only to hold. Anyway, Mr Hudson keeps him chained during the day, and until he has made his last rounds before closing the houses.'

Consequently Ellie, riding in front of the others, passed by the lighted farm-house, and pedalled on up the dark lane. Mr Maitland's woods were on either side of the road now, and the overhanging trees shut out what light remained in the sky. The river was nearer the road here, too, and the mist trailed across it, eddying in the beam of Ellie's bicycle lamp and swirling past her like grey chiffon. She slackened her pace until Roger passed and was riding ahead. It was comforting to see his rear-light going steadily before her, but even so she became increasingly depressed.

As they neared the park gates, Roger's lamp was reflected greenly in the eyes of some animal crouched on the verge. He slithered to a standstill, and the others braked sharply behind him. It was the enormous tabby cat belonging to Mr Simkin, the gamekeeper, who lived in the lodge.

They rode on in silence. Neither Mr Simkin nor the gardener nor the chauffeur could help them, but Mr Simkin was troubled.

'I don't want to worry you unnecessarily, Mr Leyland,' he said. 'But I notified Timothy Pilgrim only this morning that I've been finding traps again. I shall be doing some dawn prowling myself, soon. Don't know what it is they're after catching, really. I found two old traps set in the boss's woodland, and John Kennedy found one up on the slope of Highcomb yesterday. Might get a hare, at a pinch, but

I reckon there's only a pair of rabbits back yet in the whole place.'

He rubbed his hand up the back of his head with a rasping sound.

'I'm of the opinion that it's some lad out of the village, just doing it for devilment, and Pilgrim agrees with me,' he said. 'But even so, they're nasty things to have lying around.'

They thanked him then, and went back the way they had come. The road seemed twice as long, and the mist had turned into a thin drizzle. Ellie could feel the rain-drops hanging in a row on the edge of her fringe and tickling her forehead. Before they reached home, she couldn't be certain whether it was tears or rain that she could feel running down her chin.

While they had supper, they made their plans for the next day. Ellie was to drop off the school bus at the end of Mr Maitland's road, and walk up to go through the wood-lands there with Mr Simkin. Roger would ride up with Peter to the farm, and go round and over that end of High-comb. Jane would call at the houses in the village and make inquiries at school, to see if anyone had seen Angus since early on Monday morning. Then they would meet at a late tea-time when Daddy came back from work, and cover any ground that was left afterwards.

Mother, without mentioning it, thought that she had better ring up Riddington and Bewley police-stations in the morning to ask if anyone had reported running over a dog. Her part in the organized search, if Jane could be given a school lunch, would be to go up the hill-path which went straight out from behind the house, and do that side of Highcomb which Roger would miss.

As she lay in bed, up under the roof, Ellie heard the steady rain beating on her windows and chuckling along the guttering. She thought of Angus, soaked to the skin and shivering, hungry, and perhaps in pain, crouched on the hill-side with his leg held in a trap. He would think that they had deserted him and would feel most miserably alone. She lay wide-awake and couldn't stop her mind picturing him out there in the rain, waiting for the morning. For as long as she could remember before tonight, he had lain safe and warm in his box at the foot of her stairs, and finally she cried herself to sleep.

It would have been better, really, if Roger and Ellie hadn't gone to school at all that Tuesday. They remembered hardly anything of the day's lessons anyway, and Roger was given one hundred and fifty lines for continued and unashamed inattention. They both worked out schemes for searching the whole of their territories without covering too much of the same ground twice, and waited impatiently for four o'clock.

Eggo went up on Highcomb with Peter and Roger, after going down first to let his mother know that he'd be late. He caught them up as they left the road above the farm, and triumphantly waved a large paper bag over his head. On examination, it proved to be full of girdle scones, still warm, and firmly glued together with blackberry and apple jam. Mrs Leyland had given Roger extra sandwiches in the morning, and Peter had picked them two apples apiece in passing the Kennedys' orchard, so they felt themselves well provided for.

They moved in line abreast up the hill-side, like beaters, calling and whistling. When they came up to the flat top of

Highcomb, they moved along, and then went down in the same way. In this fashion they worked their way round the slope of the hill, up and down, until the first house-light winked up at them from Tambley. The night breeze that rises as the sun sets began to rustle in the coarse autumn grass around their feet.

Roger finally stopped. He knew that the other two would go on for as long as he did, and it was growing too dark to see anything very clearly. They said nothing, but turned and walked down again for the last time to the road. As they went through the gate which marked the boundary of Mr Kennedy's farm land, Roger turned to look up at the hill, now standing featureless against the sky.

'I don't think he can have been anywhere around, or he'd be sure to have barked,' he said, hoarse from calling, 'and really it's rather out of his usual way up here. Now he's getting on, he doesn't wander so far.'

They all thought the same thing then, but no one mentioned it—Angus, being thirteen years old, might well not stand a second night in the open, cold and damp as it was. Roger tried to push the thought from his mind.

Ellie was trying to do this too, but without success. Her time for search had been even shorter than Roger's because twilight soon crept into the woods. Mr Simkin had been very kind, and had spent the greater part of the day there, calling from time to time. When Ellie had thanked him, he had replied that it was about this season that he gave them a thorough going-through anyway to see what was what, or rather who was where. He liked to keep track of the earths, and see how some of Mr Maitland's new trees were doing.

Ellie had finished searching the remaining copses with him just as it got really dark. She found herself feeling where to put her feet, instead of looking.

'It's always surprising folk how quickly it gets dark in woodland,' Mr Simkin said, passing his little pocket torch back to Ellie. 'One minute it's afternoon, and they know just where they are, and the next minute it's night, and they're lost. I've noticed it many a time when I've been shepherding the gentry back from a shoot.'

They reached the lodge then, and Ellie realized how cold she was. She refused Mrs Simkin's offer of a cup of tea, however, explaining that she wanted to get straight back to see if Mother or Roger had had better luck than herself and Mr Simkin. Whereupon Mr Simkin disappeared round the back of the house, and returned driving his little green van, which had a wire-netting screen between the two seats and the back, and a strong smell of ferrets.

Because Mr Simkin gave Ellie a lift home, she arrived back at about the same time as Roger. He looked up eagerly as she opened the back door, but knew at once that she had found no trace of Angus either.

'What about Mother?' asked Ellie, but not hopefully.

'Nothing,' replied Roger. 'And I found nothing, and Jane found nothing. No one seems to have seen him at all. He has just vanished into thin air.'

At tea-time Daddy hesitantly asked if anything had been heard of a car accident in the district, if any dog had been run over.

'No,' said Mother quietly. 'I rang up both police-stations this morning, and they've nothing reported since Saturday. I told them that he was lost, and they'll get in touch with us if they hear anything likely.'

They sat in silence, until Daddy got up from the table, and lit his pipe.

'Well,' he said, 'there's only one thing to do now. I'll put an advertisement in the two papers.'

He crossed into the hall and came back with his pen and some paper. He wrote down the advertisement and passed it round for them to see. It was:

Lost: Border terrier, answering to name of Angus, on Monday, 14th September. Good reward for information. Leyland, Castle Tambley, Telephone—Bewley: 248.

This was the vicarage number as the Reverend Stacey was always willing to take calls for them. Daddy went round there to phone through to the Bewley and Riddington papers.

He came back into the kitchen and looked at their four unhappy faces. Mother got up slowly to do the washing-up.

'There's nothing more that we can do, I'm afraid,' said Daddy. 'The house will seem odd and empty without him, but don't forget that he was an old dog. He'd had a good life and a happy one.'

This was more than Jane could bear, and she flew to Mother to bury her face and sob into her apron.

Roger scowled at Daddy, and Ellie looked quickly down at her plate. Then she looked up slowly, a small hope growing in her eyes.

'He may have been kidnapped,' she said. Daddy looked at her sympathetically, but said nothing.

Roger turned to her sharply. 'Don't be such a complete idiot,' he said. 'Who would want to kidnap him?'

'The Mouse-man.' Ellie almost shouted it. 'Why is he always hanging round here? He was interested in Gus the first time I saw him, and he was here again on Saturday evening. You saw him yourself.'

Roger stared at her.

'Don't raise any false hopes, you two,' Daddy said seriously. 'Consider it calmly. The man was simply interested in dogs, as so many people are. What possible motive could he have? No, Ellie, I think that you can forget about your Mouse-man.'

She eyed him stubbornly, and with defiance. 'You can, but I can't,' she said emphatically. 'You haven't seen him, and he's unforgettable. I believe he must be mad. That's the only explanation I can think of.'

But, two days later, she was able to think of another one.

9

Another Use for Putty

WEDNESDAY AND THURSDAY passed quietly by. Mother moved Angus's bed from its usual corner without saying anything about it, and put it away under the stairs. Ellie remained irritable with everyone except Jane, because they all refused to believe in her kidnapping theory. Even Roger lost all interest in the Mouse-man, and told Ellie to shut up and stop whittling about him.

Thursday afternoon brought a small return of hopefulness because the 'lost' advertisement had appeared in both the local papers. Ellie went round to the vicarage before tea to inquire if there had been any telephone messages. There had not, but the Reverend Stacey promised to come round at once if he heard anything later in the evening.

They waited tea until Daddy came and had it together. 'You know, I've been feeling rather lonely these last three days,' said Mother, looking intently at the tea-cosy. 'It seems so quiet here when there's no one to talk to. What do you think about getting another dog, to be company for me?'

This suggestion was followed by a combined chorus of loud protest.

'Oh, not yet,' said Ellie. 'He may still come back. Think what he would feel like if he walked in one morning, and found another dog in his place.'

'Shall we leave it for another fortnight, then?' asked Daddy, who had obviously already talked it over with Mother. Ellie and Jane looked doubtful.

'I think it's only fair,' said Roger, 'but I don't want a puppy. I don't know what you others feel, but it would seem worse, somehow, to get a puppy.'

Ellie nodded. 'What then?' she asked. 'The only old dogs they have in Bewley cattle market are farm dogs, and you don't usually see anything but puppies in pet-shops.'

'East Hampstead,' replied Roger. This was a town thirty-five miles beyond Riddington, and about three times as big.

'Do you remember,' he continued, 'that we had an outing there, years ago, when I was in the Cubs? Well, the R.S.P.C.A. centre for the area is in East Hampstead, and we went over it. They have unclaimed strays there. They can keep so many for so long, but some of the unwanted ones are just put to sleep. If Gus doesn't turn up, we could get a grown dog there easily enough.'

'Yes,' agreed Ellie, 'that is a good idea, Roger. It wouldn't seem so much like being disloyal, would it?'

They all felt that this was the right thing to do. Jane tried to persuade them that when Angus did come back, and she was still quite convinced that he would, they really did have room for at least three unwanted dogs besides him. 'He'll be glad of the company,' she said.

'Now Janey's letting her enthusiasm run away with her,' said Mother, laughing. 'We must just wait and see what comes, and what comes at this particular moment is bed!'

'I think it better that they should have another dog more or less immediately,' said Daddy, banking down the fire with small slack, when the three of them were upstairs.

'I shall never understand where Angus went to, but I don't really believe that he will reappear now, after three days.'

'I'm afraid that I agree with you, but it seems such a long time ago that he first came to us,' said Mother, and sighed. 'Well, I think I'll go to bed myself now. Do remember to lock the back door, won't you?'

Since the attempted entry, Mother had insisted that she felt safer with the door locked, especially as Angus was no longer in the kitchen to give warning of prowlers.

So that when, four hours later, the man walked softly round the corner of the house and tried the back door, he did find it locked. He stood for a few moments looking about him uncertainly, then returned to the front of the house. This time the squeaks went unnoticed, and finally he laid another round of glass on the hedge by the gate. This time there was no boy on the stairs, and no dog to bark.

He put his hand through the hole, and moved the catch back carefully. He slowly and evenly raised the window, then stood quietly and listened, but no sound came from the village, and no sound from within the house. He took a small torch from his pocket and leant through the window into the dark room. The torch-beam showed the chrysan-themums standing on the old chest near the window. The man stretched forward and the torch snapped off. He withdrew from the open window without entering, looked carefully round once more, and moved softly away into the darkness. The house remained silent, only the curtains by the open window moving gently in the night breeze.

Mother was always up first in term-time. She went very quietly downstairs, in order to give the rest of the family a few minutes more of sleep. She stirred the ashes from the fire and placed some sticks over the red heart of it, then unlocked and opened the back door to fetch some coal. Immediately the two doors into the hall from the sitting-room and the kitchen slammed shut.

The noise woke Roger, who yawned and stretched, and rolled himself out of bed and sleep. When he went into the kitchen, he grinned at Mother, who was making up the fire and was surprised to see him.

'You're down early, dear,' she said. 'You could have had another twenty minutes.'

'Well,' he replied, 'the doors woke me. I thought you must be cross to bang them so early, and so felt it might be wise to get up sharpish.'

'Yes, I'm sorry about that,' said Mother. 'I didn't slam them really, though, they slammed themselves when I opened the back door to go to the coal-house.'

'Which were the doors that slammed, then?' asked Roger.

'The sitting-room, and the kitchen door into the hall,' she replied. 'You know I always leave the sitting-room one open because it gets so stuffy in there.'

Roger looked puzzled. 'The window must be open too, then,' he said. 'The doors wouldn't slam otherwise. They did it because you made a through draught by opening the back door.'

'No, I'm sorry if I've made it unscientific, but I closed and locked all the windows on the ground floor myself last night.' Mother turned to take the frying-pan from its hook.

'I suppose you left the kitchen door into the hall open when you came downstairs?' Roger asked.

'Yes, I think I must have done, or it wouldn't have

slammed shut, would it?' Mother smiled at him. 'It's very early in the morning to be so Sherlock Holmes-ish. Do you want two eggs?'

'Yes, please. It's illogical,' answered Roger, and went through into the sitting-room to satisfy himself that there must be a strong draught coming from somewhere.

The curtains still moved gently in the breeze by the open window, and Roger found himself for the second time staring stupidly at a hole cut in the top pane, near the catch. He stepped back into the hall.

'Come quickly,' he said, 'it's happened again.'

Mother put the frying-pan down hurriedly on the stove, and came through.

'Oh my goodness!' she said. 'This is beyond me. Go and call your father, Roger.'

Everyone came down in a rush then, and gathered in the sitting-room.

'There's the glass on the hedge again, too,' said Roger, climbing out of the window for a closer look. He was the only one who was dressed. 'Crikey! That's another use for putty! He's stuck a lump on to the window and cut round it.'

'It would be much easier to hold the piece firmly that way, I suppose,' said Daddy. 'Has he left finger-prints all over it, by any chance?'

'No,' replied Roger, peering at it closely. 'He seems to have learnt a lot since last time. He wore gloves, woollen ones, I think. There are some pieces of grey fluff stuck in the putty, anyway.'

'Now that he has succeeded,' said Mother, 'for goodness' sake let's find out what's missing. I hardly think that he can have been upstairs. Anyway, there's nothing at all worth taking there.'

'Nothing at all worth taking here, for that matter,' said
Daddy, peering into the bureau and seeing only old bills
and forgotten letters. 'What about the housekeeping
money, Mary?'

Mother went back to the kitchen and shrieked loudly.
The others ran after her to see what was wrong. They
found her standing by the stove, looking tragic, and holding up the blackened frying-pan with Roger's two shrunken
eggs very firmly stuck to the bottom of it.

'Well, you'll just have to have boiled eggs this morning,'
she said crossly. 'This pan will need soaking for about a
week and a half. Why didn't someone smell it?'

Ellie was checking the housekeeping purse, which was

kept in the drawer of the kitchen table. 'Four pounds, ten and eightpence,' she said. 'Is that right?'

'Yes,' replied Mother.

'I thought you'd find that it was,' said Ellie, looking pleased with herself. 'I know what *is* missing.'

Roger realized that she had been very quiet when they were in the sitting-room, and went quickly to have another look for himself.

Ellie followed him. 'I'll show you, if you like,' she said, with the gracious air of one who feels entitled to say 'I told you so', but refrains.

She waited until they were all there, and then picked up the vase of wooden chrysanthemums. 'The bronze one,' she said quietly.

Six chrysanthemums were there, and looked as pretty as ever, but the bronze one had disappeared.

They were not allowed to speculate for long, however, as Mother chivvied them upstairs to get washed and dressed quickly. Jane and Ellie both got into the bathroom together, because Jane stood in the bath and washed herself at the bath taps. Daddy was locked out, so he went down again to eat breakfast in his pyjamas.

'Ready, dear?' asked Mother, without looking round from making the tea.

'Ready for breakfast, yes. Ready for work, no,' replied Daddy, and Roger imagined him going to the office in orange-striped pyjamas and a green trilby, and dribbled cereal milk down his chin and his tie with laughing.

'What about Constable Pilgrim this time?' asked Mother. 'Are you going in late to work again?'

'Oh, no,' replied Daddy. 'I don't think that's necessary. We none of us saw anything, after all. I suggest that you send Jane down with a note, as before. Give him my apologies, but I really can't spare any more time.'

'Well, I suppose he can't mind,' said Mother. 'Since no one heard anything, either.'

'Tell him to come up after tea if he wants to ask us any questions,' said Daddy.

Jane and Ellie came thundering down the stairs.

'Five and a half minutes for breakfast for me,' said Ellie. 'That means seven and a half minutes for you to get washed, shaved and dressed in, Daddy.'

Daddy went thundering *up* the stairs.

'I suppose you've got a theory, then,' said Roger, grinning at Ellie. 'Are you going to make Timothy a present of it?'

'It's quite simple,' she said. 'And I expect he'll think of it for himself. That horrid man got a peculiar longing for the chrysanthemums, an obsession I suppose you could call it. He asked me if I'd sell them, and I said I wouldn't, so he tried to steal them. Angus interrupted him, and he realized that he wasn't as deaf as he appeared to be, so he tried to decoy him away on Saturday. You interrupted him then, so he tried again on Monday morning when he knew that Mother was alone and busy, and succeeded. Then he was finally able to get in last night, and took the bronze chrysanthemum. I wish I could understand, though, why he only took that one.' Ellie finished theorizing on a wistful note.

'Perhaps he thought that just one wouldn't be missed,' suggested Jane, helpfully.

'It's a lot of ballyhoo,' argued Roger. 'Why ever should he want a cheap little wooden chrysanthemum? You're basing your whole argument on the fact that the

Mouse-man is potty. Well, I don't think that he is; he just looks a bit odd. A lot of people do, but they aren't all potty.'

The jangling of bicycle bells sounded from the road outside, as Daddy came slowly down the stairs doing his tie up.

The argument came to an end.

Small Dog with Black Ears

JANE AGAIN TOOK the message to Constable Pilgrim, who found her a liquorice bootlace to eat whilst he read it.

'Now, this seems to be becoming a habit,' he said, smiling. 'And I do hope that your Roger's not playing a game with Mr Leyland and myself. We haven't the time to be engaging in practical jokery.'

Jane hastily denied this, and replied that it was the Mouse-man. Whereupon P.C. Pilgrim laughed almost as much as Roger had done, and sent her off to school with what remained of the liquorice, and a black tongue.

He arrived at the house just as Mother was rolling out pastry for a treacle-tart, and she felt obliged to leave it while she answered his questions. Since this took longer than she had anticipated, the pastry had begun to feel elderly and unwanted by the time she got back to it. Consequently, treacle-tart that evening was not a success although, as it happened, no one was worried about it.

Constable Pilgrim again measured the hole in the window, and informed Mother with mock solemnity that this one was only a quarter of an inch larger than the last, but two inches more to the right. He could hardly bring himself to believe that nothing at all was missing, since the window had been found open. When Mother pointed out that one wooden chrysanthemum had disappeared, he was puzzled and made a note of it.

'Although I can't see what possible connexion or significance it could have,' he said. 'Can you be quite certain that all seven of them were there yesterday, Mrs Leyland?'

'Well no, I suppose not,' she replied. 'It could have been missing for several days in fact, and I wouldn't have noticed. Perhaps one of the children will be more help, though. Ellie sometimes comes in here to do her homework.'

She promised to keep them at home after tea, so that he could come up again then, and went with him to the gate. He wrapped his handkerchief carefully round the glass and the lump of putty, and said good-bye. Mother went back to her pastry.

Roger had had a most satisfying day at school. This second, and more successful, burglary had once more made him the centre of attention in his form, and numerous lurid sequels to it were discussed at break. Most boys thought that the thief must have been disturbed again, and that it would be a case of third time lucky. Simon Wilkins expressed the opinion that the Leylands' house must have been built over the site of some ancient buried treasure, the whereabouts of which had at last been discovered by the Mouse-man, who now assumed sinister proportions.

'Then why ever did he ask my sister if he could buy the wooden chrysanthemums?' asked Roger, unwillingly beginning to believe this astonishing and unlikely explanation.

'To have an excuse for gaping through your front window, of course,' promptly replied Simon Wilkins, with scorn. 'When you wake up in the morning, you'll probably find all those floorboards up, a great hole dug in the foundations, and the Saxon treasure-cache emptied.'

So he effectively silenced Roger and the others, who gazed at him in admiration. In the art of conjuring up wild stories at a moment's notice, Simon Wilkins was their acknowledged master. The only one who did not share in this belief was Mrs Wilkins, who complained bitterly that Simon did not know even the basic difference between fact and fiction. This was after he inadvertently broke his bedroom window while stunning an imaginary, though none the less dangerous, murderer with a stool.

Now Peter, Roger and Eggo were more or less home. They had stopped on the crest of the hump-backed bridge over the River Ridding to discuss the possibility of having their home-made rowing boat watertight and river-worthy before Christmas. Peter was expressing rather a gloomy view of the whole undertaking, and saying that he didn't think that the planks were thick enough, when a car hooter behind them made them hastily string out in a line by the bridge wall.

It was a black and glossy police patrol-car that had come down from Tambley unnoticed. The driver raised his hand in salute as he went past, the engine scarcely audible above the murmur of the strongly running river. The car disappeared, going at a leisurely pace towards Riddington.

The three of them pedalled fast up the hill to Tambley, and parted as usual in the village. As Roger came up to the vicarage, the Reverend Stacey came hurrying out of his front door.

'Roger!' he called, catching sight of him over the hedge. 'There's a phone call for you, an inquiry about Angus.'

Roger dropped his bike immediately on to the verge and followed the Vicar quickly into his hall.

The voice of the caller was a brisk one, and identified itself as belonging to a police constable.

'I am speaking from a Riddington call-box,' went on the voice. 'I picked up a terrier with no collar near the Bewley cross-roads a few moments ago. He ran past the patrol-car which I was driving into Riddington.'

'We saw you,' interrupted Roger.

'On the bridge? Well, I'm not up to much in dog identification,' continued the voice, 'and I don't know a Border terrier when I see one. I thought it better to check with you before bringing him over to Tambley. Is it a small dog with black ears? A sort of yellowy-brown? He certainly seems to be an Angus, even if he's not a Border terrier.'

'Oh yes, he is. That's him all right,' Roger shouted enthusiastically into the telephone. 'That's him. Brown eyes, and going grey on his face, and fairly thin.'

'Four legs and a tail too,' said the policeman, 'not to mention two whole ears. I'll believe you then. We'll be right over.'

Roger more or less threw the receiver back on the rest, just remembered to thank the Vicar, and, forgetting his bicycle altogether, ran home.

Ellie had arrived there before him today, and was doing Jane's hair up in miniature and stringy plaits at her own request. 'It's not nearly long enough yet,' she said. 'Hold still!'

Jane was hopping up and down, impatient to see if Mr Catlin was in sight, bringing yet another new window-pane to be fitted. They turned as Roger opened the door.

'Gus is on his way,' he said, grinning from ear to ear. 'They've found him. Where's Mother? He'll be here at any moment now, in a police car.'

Jane shot up the stairs, shouting at the top of her voice, the plaits unravelling as she went.

'Angus?' asked Ellie incredulously. 'Where is he? Who found him?'

Mother and Jane arrived together, and Mother sent Ellie under the stairs to fetch Angus's bed out.

'There was a phone call just as I was coming past the vicarage. The policeman in the patrol-car saw him running somewhere near Bewley cross-roads and he's not got his collar on. Who's coming out to the gate?'

They all went, of course, although Mother tried to make them wait long enough to put their coats on.

'The car's bound to be at least another ten minutes,' she said.

It was longer than that, but in the meantime Mr Catlin arrived, looking surprised to see a reception committee waiting, apparently for him. Then he had to listen to three versions of two explanations about Angus and the cut window, all at the same time, and so gratefully accepted Mother's offer of a quiet cup of tea in the kitchen. 'Until all this excitement has died down,' she said.

Roger saw the police car first, when he went to fetch his bike, which was still lying on the grass outside the vicarage. The policeman arrived at the Leylands' house just after he did, and reached across to open the passenger's door and let Angus out. Mother came round from the back door then, and everyone talked to and hugged and patted Angus at more or less the same time. He barked and panted and wagged the whole of himself as well as his tail, and then ran up Mother's front to lick her face vigorously.

The policeman turned the car, and wound his window down as he came back.

'I can take it, then, that this is the right dog?' he asked,

leaning out and smiling. 'He's been lost for five days, hasn't he? Looks remarkably well-fed.'

'Yes,' replied Mother. 'He does. I really can't understand it, unless some child has been keeping him secretly, and he only managed to get out this afternoon. Anyway, thank you so much for bringing him over.'

'A pleasure, madam,' said the policeman, and raised his hand again in salute as the car moved away.

Mother put Angus down in the road and he began to run in wild circles round them, using his tail as a balance when cornering and barking madly at the top of his voice. Mr Catlin came out, having finished his tea, and laughed so much at him that Angus ran between his legs and in at the back door, looking for his water. Mother and Ellie followed him in to get his two bowls out and filled. Jane and Roger stayed behind to explain to Mr Catlin about the putty stuck to the glass, and Roger asked him what he thought of Simon Wilkins's theory about buried Saxon treasure.

Mr Catlin roared with laughter again, and said that he didn't think much of it, but couldn't exactly say that it was wrong until the whole house had been demolished and the foundations dug up.

'Don't reckon your father would approve, lad,' he said.

Jane went down to wait at the bus stop for the Bewley bus, so that she could tell Daddy the good news immediately. When he arrived at the house there was a large and various noise again, made up of barks, and chatter, and the kettle whistling in the middle of it. They had tea, and then Mr Catlin came round to say that he had finished, and that he hoped for their sakes that he wouldn't be seeing them again yet awhile.

As he went out of the front gate, Constable Pilgrim came in through it and wished him a cheerful 'good evening'.

He was very pleased to see that Angus had returned safely, and Angus was equally pleased to see him. Roger explained again how the policeman had picked him up when he was running near the Bewley cross-roads.

Only Ellie was positive that all seven chrysanthemums had been in the vase before the second hole had been cut in the window, and even she couldn't think why she was positive. She said that she just was.

Constable Pilgrim closed his little note-book and shook his head mournfully. 'Feminine intuition is all very well,' he said, 'but it doesn't look good on paper: "When the witness was asked why she was so certain of the facts, she replied that she just was." Well, a female judge might take that as a reason, but we've none of them yet, thank goodness.'

He helped Roger with algebra problems for ten minutes, and then stood up. Roger tried to tempt him to stay longer by offering him a slice of what he called cast-iron-and-treacle-tart, but it was politely refused.

'I mean no offence to you, Mrs Leyland, of course,' he said, 'but I have to go out with Mr Simkin now, to look round for that poacher, and they do say that he travels fastest who travels alone.'

11

A Man Digging

ANGUS WAS HOME again and everything was as usual. Rain came with October and seemed determined to stay until 5th November in order to ruin the bonfires, but on the last day of the month relented. When Ellie woke up in the morning, she thought that she must have been singing in her sleep, because she felt so tremendously happy. She stretched and yawned, and suddenly remembered why. First of all, it was half-term. Secondly, it was only Saturday and four whole days of holiday lay in front of her. Thirdly, the sun was shining and the sky filling the high window opposite her bed was clear and blue.

'Enough blue sky to make a whole fleet of sailors a pair of trousers,' thought Ellie, and dressed quickly.

Roger was eating an enormous bowl of porridge encrusted with brown sugar. Ellie sat down beside him.

'Cream!' she exclaimed, and seized the jug. 'Sunshine *and* cream! It's going to be a good day. I can feel it in my bones.'

'Yes, I got the cream from Mr Robertson as a sort of celebration for sunshine,' said Mother. 'I take it that you want porridge this morning too, Ellie?'

'Oh yes, please,' she replied, and looked sideways at Roger's plate. 'Will there be enough for Daddy and Jane, though?'

'I knew it would be popular this morning, so I made double,' said Mother. 'Anyway, Jane's had hers. She's in the garden somewhere.'

Daddy creaked slowly down the stairs and came blinking into the sunlight.

'Sleep-walking again, he is,' said Ellie.

'Was that you or the stairs creaking?' asked Roger.

Daddy batted them both on the head with a table-mat, and stuck his own out of the back door to wake himself up.

'Whatever is Jane doing in that apple-tree?' he asked.

Ellie and Roger stood up at the table to peer out of the window.

'She's making a nest for herself, or something,' replied Mother. 'She did ask me first, because she wanted to borrow the clothes-line. I gave her your garden twine instead, John.'

'Well, knock me down with a feather! Did you ever!' exclaimed Daddy. 'Why my garden twine but not your clothes-line, may I ask?'

'You haven't used that twine for weeks, and I shall need the line this morning,' said Mother, ladling porridge into a bowl and quickly cooling it with cream to stop Daddy talking. It didn't.

'I've been planning for weeks past to use that twine this very afternoon,' said Daddy round a mouthful of porridge. 'Ow!' he stood up quickly to get a glass of water, and turned the tap on too hard, so that the water bounced up from the bottom of the glass and showered all over him. 'Now I'm hot and cold in patches,' he complained.

'Serves you right for grumbling, then,' said Ellie, and went quickly out into the garden to avoid the dish-cloth.

She came back carrying the twine. 'Jane finds that she

doesn't need it now,' she explained. 'She has used six of your pea-sticks instead.'

Daddy rolled his eyes in horror, but couldn't say anything because his mouth was full of porridge again.

'The lesser of two evils,' said Mother.

'And it's not a nest, either,' said Ellie; 'it's going to be a little round house, like a harvest-mouse makes, and she says she's going to hibernate.'

'I'd like her to,' said Daddy, 'it would be cheaper for me, but they wouldn't let her do it, you know. They'd all be round here in no time—school-attendance officer, police, N.S.P.C.C., reporters and photographers. It won't work, so she may as well give me back my pea-sticks.'

Ellie finished her breakfast quickly, and went upstairs to do her bed and Roger's, a job which she liked to get done early on Saturdays, because it was clean-sheets day. She hated changing sheets because she had to run round and round the bed and kept knocking her legs on the frame.

Roger and Daddy were still eating steadily when she went down into the kitchen.

'What are you doing this morning, Roger?' asked Ellie.

'Going down to Hudsons' with Peter,' he replied. 'We want to get on with the boat, and it's not progressing very well just now. It's not going to look like any other boat in the world. It will be unique and we shall have to patent it, I expect.'

'*I* expect that the only way in which it will be at all unique will be that it floats underwater, instead of on the surface,' replied Ellie, a little cross now because she would have to go out on her own. The nearest of her friends lived on a farm five miles from Riddington, too far to go on a Saturday morning.

'If that is so,' said Mother, peacefully, 'it will be the first submarine to be made from old wood by three school-boys, and will be in all the Sunday newspapers. Can you go straight down to the shop for me, Ellie, please, to collect the bread? Then you could ride down with Roger as far as the farm, and pick me some fresh haws.'

Ellie grew more cheerful again as she walked down into the village and she found only one other customer in Betty's shop, which was a miracle for Saturday. It was Mrs Simkin, and she was getting up to date with the village news.

'Yes, Timothy's gone into Riddington this morning,' said Betty, as Ellie opened the door. 'He's gone to have a conference with Inspector Charles, so Miss Pilgrim was telling me. August 27th it was, that Mr Maitland's silver was taken, and here we are near November and they've found nothing at all.'

Ellie waited till all Mrs Simkin's groceries had been collected, and then carried an armful of tins outside for her to pack into the old basket on her bicycle.

Even when this was full, and with a string bag hanging on one handlebar and a paper carrier-bag hanging on the other, there were still some tins and the potatoes left over.

'Bother it then,' said Mrs Simkin. 'It looks as if I've been too hopeful altogether this morning, and I need all this stuff too, because we've got Frank's brother's family coming over for Sunday. I'll leave them in with Betty and toddle back this afternoon for them, that's all.'

'Well, I've nothing to do this morning, Mrs Simkin,' said Ellie, pausing at the door. 'And I was coming down your lane anyway, after haws. I'll bring them for you in my bike basket.'

'Now that is kind of you, my dear,' said Mrs Simkin, thankfully. 'I've certainly got enough to do this afternoon, without coming back here. I'll have some nice creamy coffee and a slice or two of seed-cake waiting for you, and we can have a little chat.'

Ellie left the tins and the potatoes in the shop while she went home to fetch her bike. Roger was almost ready to come out, so she sat on the table to wait for him.

'There's nothing that gives me quite the same pleasure as watching other people work,' remarked Ellie, swinging her legs.

Roger was cleaning her shoes and Jane's and his own. He did this instead of making his bed, which he considered was not a man's job. He finished, and packed the brushes away in the box.

'Aren't you going to wash your hands? You look like a sweep,' said Ellie.

'Crikey, no! I'm only going boat-building after all—not to tea with the Lord Mayor,' replied Roger, and went round to get his bike.

They stopped at the shop for the groceries, and then rode on through the village to turn down the Riddington road towards Mr Maitland's estate. Roger left Ellie at the Hudsons' farm gate, and she heard Sam's chain rattle as he stepped growling from his kennel to see who had come. Ellie rode on alone.

The lane went into the woodland and sunlight flickered on her face as she passed under the trees. There were patches of sunshine and shadow, golden and grey, and Ellie was warm and cold alternately. The Hall was farther round the slope of Highcomb Hill, so a little lower than the village, and she was able to free-wheel most of the way.

She heard a pheasant's harsh honking call echo through the woods, and the yellow leaves floated gently down as the breeze tossed the heads of the trees above her. Her tyres fizzed quietly along the road and Ellie felt as if she were fizzing too, happy because Saturday stretched out before her.

As she approached the lodge gates, she whistled to let the dogs know that she was coming, so that they in turn could let Mrs Simkin know that she was coming, and that it was time to put the milk on for the coffee. They did, and she looked over the hedge at them as she went by. The four black labradors stood barking in their pen, but with their tails lazily waving to and fro to show that they knew that anyone arriving so noisily could not mean much harm. The two terriers yapped hysterically, bouncing up and down like energetic rubber balls in order to see out through the wire netting. Ellie shouted to them, and the noise became less as three of the labradors sat down and were quiet.

Mrs Simkin was pouring the coffee into the cups as Ellie pushed open the door, her arms full of tins and potatoes. A brown and yellow seed-cake stood on the table, as full of caraway seeds as crumbs.

It was Ellie's favourite, because it was the most lingering kind of cake she knew. For hours after eating it, you kept finding seeds hidden away in your teeth, and so had a continuous taste of caraway to enjoy. The barking of the terriers ceased abruptly, and Mrs Simkin nodded in their direction. 'That'll be Frank,' she said. 'If he's not around to stop them, they carry on for a good half-hour after whoever it was has left.'

Ellie laughed. 'Well, you certainly won't find anyone cutting a hole in *your* front window,' she said.

Mrs Simkin agreed with that, and cut a fat slice out of the cake for her. They talked busily for about twenty minutes, or rather Mrs Simkin did, because Ellie preferred to listen when possible. Then Mr Simkin came in carrying a billhook, and looking for his greasy rag to wipe it down with. He smiled at Ellie, and reached over to cut himself an immense piece of cake.

'I thought it was you, Ellie,' he said. 'I heard you shouting to the dogs. Those nipper terriers make more noise than a pack of hounds, but we've got so as we don't hear them now.' He looked at the clock.

'Have you got to be straight back, or have you got an hour or so to spare?' he asked.

Ellie looked at the clock too. It was only half past ten, and she still had one half of a free morning to enjoy.

'I've just been trimming a nice ash-sapling down,' continued Mr Simkin. 'My old vermin pole in the river-end wood is rotten, and I'm taking this one over there now. Want to come along?'

'Oh, yes,' said Ellie, shaking the cake-crumbs from her lap into the hearth.

She enjoyed looking at Mr Simkin's vermin poles, where hung the bodies of the pests he shot in the woods, although the squeamish side of her was always a little disgusted. You had to try to forget about the smell. You never knew what you were going to find there; twice she had seen cats hanging up that had been left as strays and run wild. Once there had been a badger, and there were usually several carrion crows, one or two jays, magpies, and a stoat or a weasel.

Ellie thanked Mrs Simkin for the coffee, who thanked her back for the tins, and followed Mr Simkin outside.

'I think we'll take Nero along with us,' he said. 'The more handling he gets the better. He's still a deal too noisy.'

Nero was one of the black labradors, not yet two years old, and was being trained for Mr Maitland's use as a gun dog.

As Mr Simkin approached their large pen, all the dogs sat up expectantly, but when he called only Nero to him, the three older dogs flopped down again with a sigh. Almost at once, Nero was reprimanded for flourishing round their legs and barking, but redeemed himself by waiting quietly at the roadside until told to cross.

'He's a good dog when he sets his mind to it,' said Mr Simkin, 'but it's not second nature to him yet. A few months should see a lot of difference in him.'

They left the road and the Hall gates at their back, and went down a ride which led through the woods to the river. There had been a number of trees felled in the lower woodland in the early spring and they had been dragged up this ride in chains behind the tractor. The deep grass-grown ruts made walking a matter for concentration, and Ellie remarked that she was glad that they weren't in any hurry.

'Yes,' replied Mr Simkin, 'you could pretty soon break an ankle trying to run up here. By next summer they'll have finished felling, and then the boss will have the plough and the harrow in for sure. This is no good for a horse.'

Nero was following quietly at heel, and Mr Simkin suggested that Ellie might like to see an old fox-earth that a badger had recently moved into after a thorough spring-clean, the traces of which were still visible around the sett. He left the ash-sapling leaning against an oak-tree, and

turned left into the wood. They were not far from the river now.

Thinking about it afterwards, Ellie could never be sure which of the three of them saw the man first. Probably they all saw him at the same time, because he was so suddenly there. They had been walking in single file along a path which crossed a small clearing, choked with high brown bracken, small saplings and elderberry bushes. The man was digging amongst the roots of an enormous beech, and whirled round to meet them when he heard Mr Simkin's exclamation of surprise.

Ellie knew even as she stared at him that she would never forget the look on his face, and that years later she would remember every detail of the scene before her as if she had a photograph printed in her mind. The green and yellow woodland stood behind him, and the smooth grey trunk of the great beech-tree towered above them all. The spade was half raised, clodded with damp black earth, and the man was shivering. Ellie saw the look of terror that seemed frozen on his face, but which changed to desperation as he swung the spade behind him.

Then Mr Simkin pushed her sideways into the bracken, and a great many things seemed to be happening at the same time. When she pulled herself to her feet, she saw the man staggering away towards the river and Nero hanging almost off the ground with his teeth in the man's arm. He swung the arm with an effort hard against a tree trunk, and kicked the dog as he fell from him. Then he ran wildly away into the wood, bulldozing through bushes and bracken.

It was the Mouse-man.

12

Fire, Police or Ambulance?

THE WOOD WAS very silent after he had gone. Ellie stood perfectly still, clutching bracken in both her hands, and she didn't seem able to let it go. Then she saw Nero get up from under the trees and stand shaking his head. He looked round uncertainly as if wondering how he had got there, and if anyone was with him. Ellie called, and he turned and came towards her, limping badly, but with his tail waving.

Her hands came to life then, and let go of the bracken fronds. She ran over to the beech-tree and knelt beside Mr Simkin, who lay quietly on his back, the spade by his side. Blood welled slowly from a deep cut which stretched from his ear back to the crown of his head. A pale beech leaf fluttered down from the tree above and lay on his cheek. Ellie brushed it away automatically. Nero drooped his tail between his legs and moaned softly in his throat. Ellie came suddenly to life.

She took off her mac and then her cardigan and placed them over Mr Simkin, tucking them firmly underneath him. She took off his tie and found his handkerchief, which she folded into a long pad. She fixed this in place over the cut as best she could with the tie and then pulled out the belt from the loops of her mac. Nero came willingly when she spoke to him, and stood quietly while she threaded the belt through his collar and tied it round an exposed tree root.

'Now, don't pull very hard, please,' she said to him, 'or that knot will come undone. I want you to be here for company for him when he wakes.'

Nero lay down at once, as if he understood, and Ellie turned and ran back through the clearing to the ride. The ash-sapling still leant against the oak-tree, marking the entrance to the little path. It seemed at least an hour ago since Mr Simkin had left it there, and yet it could not have been much longer than ten minutes.

The wood became larger and grew more silent as Ellie ran through it, and her heart became larger too, but grew more noisy. It hammered away all through her body, in her stomach, in her lungs, in her head, and thundered in her ears. She stumbled and leapt over the deep ruts, and the ride grew longer instead of shorter. So she was running almost automatically, with her head down and a shooting pain in her lungs, when she found the gate into the road standing solidly before her.

The calves of her legs began to tremble violently as soon as she stopped running, and she walked slowly across the road, shouting to Mrs Simkin, and wearily lifted her bicycle from the wall.

'What is it?' asked Mrs Simkin sharply, grasping the handlebars.

Ellie told her in two sentences, and Mrs Simkin ran back for some water when she realized that Ellie would have to go off again to the telephone. She had wheeled her bike through to the house drive when Mrs Simkin brought the water back to her.

'No, it's no use going up there.' The colour had left

Mrs Simkin's face. 'You'll have to go right into Tambley,' she continued. 'Mr Maitland's up in Scotland grouse-shooting. Mrs Bassett's on holiday. The big house is locked up.'

Ellie tried to reassure her. 'The telephone-box is only at the top of the Riddington road,' she said. 'It'll not take me more than eight minutes. You go and collect Arthur and Mr Coles, and get them to carry Mr Simkin up here to you. I'll send the doctor here, and tell the police. Then I'll ask Mr Hudson and his worker to bring me on in the car, and we three will go down to meet the other two and help them back.'

Arthur, the gardener, came from his house then to see what was happening and Ellie explained just where she had left Mr Simkin, and that the cut sapling marked the place to turn off the main ride. He ran back to fetch Mr Coles, the chauffeur, from his garage, and Ellie set off towards Tambley, ignoring the ache which returned to her lungs, feeling her legs forcing down the pedals like pistons.

After laboured running over grass-covered ruts, she seemed to be almost flying over the road on her bicycle. Trees and telegraph poles seemed to flash past and in only a few minutes, so it seemed, she was going by Mr Hudson's farm. There was no one in sight there, and Ellie dared not stop. She went on and turned left up the hill to Tambley and threw her bicycle, with the wheels spinning, down on the grass outside the telephone-box. There had been a great outcry when it had been placed here, instead of in the centre of the village, but now Ellie was glad of it.

A large notice hanging in the box instructed her to dial 999 in an emergency, and to ask for the service required— fire, police or ambulance. She had dialled 999 even before the door had closed in slow motion behind her. The brisk voice of the operator said, 'Emergency—which service do you require?'

'Ambulance,' said Ellie, and almost immediately found herself speaking to the casualty department at Bewley Hospital. 'Ten minutes,' said the voice there, enigmatically, when she had explained herself, and the receiver clicked sharply in her ear. She replaced it, and pushed hard at the door. After a brief struggle with it, she had one foot outside, when she remembered the police.

She dialled again, and this time found herself speaking to the officer on duty at Riddington police-station. Again she explained herself, this time more fully. The policeman was noticeably less brisk than the nurse had been.

'We'll be with you in twenty minutes,' he said, after some half-heard conversation in the duty-room.

'And you're an optimist,' muttered Ellie as she threw herself at the door and almost fell full-length into the road. The makers of doors of telephone-boxes always seemed to take their work too seriously, she thought as she bent to pick up her bicycle.

Now that she had more time to think, she began puzzling about the connexion which she felt must be there, between the Mouse-man's breaking into their house and digging secretly in Mr Maitland's woods. She was too excited to reason it out logically, though, and forgot about it as she turned down into the Hudsons' farm to find someone to help carry Mr Simkin.

Mr Hudson's worker was in Riddington, buying poultry-feed, so it was Mr Hudson, Roger, Peter and Eggo who climbed into the farm truck with Ellie, and arrived a very few minutes later outside the lodge gates.

'Is it any use taking the truck down the ride, Ellie?' asked Mr Hudson.

'I should say that the ruts are too deep,' she replied. 'It would shake Mr Simkin too much; it's bad enough walking.'

Ellie stayed behind to keep Mrs Simkin company while the other four hurried away to relieve Mr Coles and Arthur. They were already in sight, coming slowly back up the ride, when the ambulance pulled in by the gate. There was no doctor in Castle Tambley, so that most people were registered with a doctor in Bewley, and Ellie knew the one that had come in the ambulance by sight. He was a young man with bright ginger hair, his face covered with freckles, and he smiled reassuringly at Mrs Simkin as he asked for details of the accident.

'Well, it wasn't an accident, precisely,' said Ellie. 'A man hit him on the head, and knocked him out.'

'Police case then,' said the doctor. 'Is the head cut?'

'Yes, quite a deep cut, about five inches long, and it was bleeding quite fast when I left him,' Ellie replied.

'Stitches. Possible transfusion,' said the doctor briskly. He turned to the driver.

'Might take him in. Might not. Soon see.' Ellie smiled at him, thinking that he talked as a note-book would, if it did.

He smiled back at her, and the ambulance driver crossed the road to open the gate for the others. They had made the usual amateur's stretcher out of three jackets threaded by their sleeves on to two strong poles. Ellie noticed that one of these was the vermin pole itself. Mr Hudson and Eggo carried the front, and Mr Coles and Roger carried the back of the stretcher. Peter staggered behind carrying

Nero, whose leg had swelled up badly, and Arthur was nowhere in sight. Mr Coles saw Ellie looking for him.

'He's gone back to stay by that hole until the police come,' he said. 'He thought that the man might come back, and says that if he does, he wants to be there to give *him* a clip with the spade.'

The doctor looked up sharply from his examination of Mr Simkin.

'Spade?' he asked. 'Was this done with a spade?'

'Yes,' replied Ellie, 'the man was digging.'

'Alters the case then. Better take him to Bewley. Never can tell with soil. Tetanus, you know.'

Mrs Simkin clutched at his arm, and he patted her in a comfortable way. 'Sorry,' he said, smiling. 'Didn't mean to frighten you. No risk if he's with us. I'll inject him with anti-tetanus as soon as we get to the hospital. You'd better come along too, and be there when he comes round. Must have been a very hard knock to keep him unconscious so long.'

Mr Simkin was carefully transferred to the bed in the ambulance, and the doctor cleaned the cut with the hot water which Mrs Simkin had ready. Then he closed the doors from the inside, and Mrs Simkin got in beside the driver. The remaining six stood and watched the ambulance start smoothly away and disappear under the trees.

Then Ellie had to describe exactly what had happened to the others, and Roger was as puzzled as she had been when he heard that it was the Mouse-man again. Peter had set Nero down by the roadside, and was rubbing his arms vigorously.

'That dog is as heavy as his master,' he said, 'or practically, anyway. Where are we going to take him?'

Mr Coles looked doubtful.

'Well,' he said, 'Arthur and I can manage the other labradors and the two terriers, but I'm no good with sick dogs.'

'Nor me,' said Mr Hudson, 'I've no confidence where dogs are concerned.'

'Chicken-hearted,' said Eggo, grinning.

'You're no eggspert yourself,' said Roger, moving out of range.

Ellie frowned at them for being frivolous, and felt Nero's swollen leg very gently, while he watched her anxiously.

'I don't think it's broken,' she said, 'but it was badly bruised when that man swung him against the tree.'

'I'll take him home with me,' said Peter. 'Dad will know what to do. Can you give me a lift up, Mr Hudson?'

'Yes, I'll do that. What about you two?' Mr Hudson turned to Roger and Ellie.

'I'd better stay, and take the police down,' said Ellie, 'and anyway my mac and cardigan are still there.'

'I'll stay with you then,' said Roger, 'but can you let Mother know that we'll be late in, and ask her to put our dinners in the oven, Mr Hudson?'

Peter jumped into the back of the truck and Mr Hudson handed Nero up to him.

'I'll do that with pleasure,' he replied. Mr Coles went back to his garage and Mr Hudson drove off to Tambley. As he turned out of the lane into the Riddington road, a police car turned in.

'They'll not have long to wait then,' he said.

13

The Mouse-hole

ROGER WAS SITTING on the gate whistling, and Ellie was doing a private jig on the grass, trying to keep warm. Now that the excitement had died down a little, she realized how cold she was.

The police car drew up beside them and a sergeant and the driver got out and slammed the doors. The sergeant looked at Ellie in silence for a moment.

'Are you a Spartan, young lady?' he inquired gravely. 'Or have you recently come over from Baffin Island?'

Ellie imagined a map of the world in her mind, and began to search feverishly on it for Baffin Island.

'Up at the top,' suggested the sergeant helpfully. 'In the Arctic. What I mean is, where's your coat?'

Ellie was relieved that this was all he did mean. 'Oh,' she said, 'I put my mac and my cardigan over Mr Simkin to try and keep him warm. They are still down in the wood, I think. They're not up here, anyway, so they must be.'

'Give the young lady the car-rug, until we get there,' said the sergeant to the driver.

He brought a large black rug out from the back seat of the car and Ellie wound herself up in it.

'You look exactly like an Hungarian peasant going to a funeral,' said Roger, climbing down from the gate and laughing at her.

Ellie felt like asking him how he knew, since he had never even seen a Hungarian peasant, let alone one going to a funeral, but she felt that they ought to be reasonably polite whilst they were with the policemen, so she ignored him.

'Do you want me to show you where it all happened?' she asked.

'Yes, if you will, please,' said the sergeant. 'And we should like a formal statement from you later on.'

Roger opened the gate for them, and Ellie explained about vermin poles as they went along. When they reached the place where the ash-sapling had leant against the oak-tree until taken for use in the stretcher, they found Arthur leaning there instead, smoking.

'I'm glad you've not dawdled,' he said. 'I was in the middle of making up my hot-house boiler when Ellie here brought us news of the accident, and I left the draught-door wide open. If I don't go off straight away, the grape-vine in there will get ideas about being a tropical creeper and start running about on the roof. I haven't seen anything of the digging man, and I left the spade where it was.'

The sergeant thanked him, and said that he would perhaps be round to see him and Mr Coles later in the afternoon. Arthur hurried away up the ride, and Ellie led the way across the clearing to the beech-tree.

Her mac and cardigan lay in a heap by the spade, and the macintosh belt was among the roots of the tree, where she had left Nero tied. The spade lay a little way from the hole, which was about three feet deep, and a small patch of blood showed where Mr Simkin had been lying.

Ellie picked up her cardigan and her mac, shook out the leaf mould from them, and put them on.

The constable was looking carefully at the ground beyond the hole, in the direction of the river. He wandered in and out of the bushes and then returned to them.

'If I could get B.P. down here fairly soon, Sergeant, I think that there is a good chance of picking up the trail,' he said. 'Then at least we shall know in which direction he was heading.'

The sergeant nodded.

'B.P.?' said Roger. 'Is that what you call Constable Pilgrim? I didn't know his name began with a B; I thought it was Timothy.'

'Is he an especially good tracker, then?' asked Ellie. 'Of course, he is the scout-master, isn't he?'

The sergeant smiled broadly, and the constable stared at the two of them for a moment before beginning to laugh with a secret sort of enjoyment.

'Oh, no,' he said. 'I don't mean Constable Pilgrim from Tambley. I mean the station police-dog, B.P. He's an Alsatian.'

'Could you tell us what B.P. means, then?' asked Roger.

'Yes,' said the constable, laughing again. 'It's short for Baden-Powell, because he is our chief scout, and prepared for anything.'

The sergeant had bent down to examine the spade.

'Does the doctor know that Mr Simkin was hit by a spade?' he asked.

'Yes,' Ellie replied. 'He said he would give him an anti-tetanus injection right away.'

'That's all right, then,' said the sergeant, standing up. 'Now, can you show me exactly what happened?'

'Yes,' said Ellie. 'Can Roger be Mr Simkin? You'll have to imagine Nero walking at heel.'

The two policemen stood under the beech-tree, on the far side of the hole, and saw how suddenly Roger and Ellie appeared round the elderberry bushes which stood between the tree and the clearing. Then the sergeant was Mr Simkin instead of Roger, and finally Ellie showed them where he had pushed her sideways into the bracken.

'Then the next thing that I saw was the Mouse-man running away over there'—she pointed towards the river—'with Nero hanging on to his left arm. He knocked Nero's head on that holly-tree and kicked him as he was falling.'

The sergeant looked at her sharply when she called the previously apparently unknown man 'the Mouse-man', but left his questions until later.

'How did you fall in the bracken?' he asked. 'Did you just fall on your hands and knees, or did you go full-length on the ground?'

'It was a hard push,' explained Ellie. 'And I wasn't expecting it. I fell right over and then rolled a little way. I didn't see anything of what happened to Mr Simkin, but only what I have just told you.'

'I see,' replied the sergeant, and walked over to the hole. He stared down at it reflectively, then turned suddenly and looked at Ellie in a serious way.

'Now then, why did you call this person the Mouse-man a moment ago?' he asked. 'Was it just because he looked like a mouse?'

'Yes,' said Ellie. 'That's why I called him it in the first place. He's got very pale hair and very pale eyes, and a twitchy sort of a nose. I have seen him once before and so has Roger.'

The sergeant was looking at her very steadily. 'Where was that?' he asked.

Ellie explained quickly about her meeting with him in the road, and how Roger had found him talking to Angus exactly a week ago. She looked sideways at Roger, and explained her theory about the two attempted house entries.

'I don't think that the second one was just "attempted",' she said. 'Although everyone else seems to. I think it was successful and that he wanted the chrysanthemums all along, although I can't imagine why he should.'

Roger was grinning broadly, but the sergeant looked thoughtfully at the hole again.

'Hmn,' he said, and poked at the side of it with his shoe.

No one said anything then, and Roger waited in a hungry silence for further developments. He didn't want to miss anything that happened, but he didn't want to miss his dinner either.

The sergeant suddenly picked up the spade by the iron part just above the blade, where the wooden shaft was fitted in. He peered intently at the handle of it.

'I don't suppose that there will be any prints on this,' he said. 'But better safe than sorry. Can you dig with it, holding it just here on the metal, Elliot?'

The constable stepped over and took the spade from him.

'Yes,' he replied, after a few experimental thrusts into the leaf mould. 'But not for too long. It feels like a very top-heavy and unbalanced trowel.'

The sergeant nodded and turned to Ellie and Roger.

'I ought, strictly speaking, to send you home now, just as it becomes interesting. Do you realize that?' he said. 'But I suppose that you would prefer to stay?'

'Oh yes, please,' said Ellie.

Roger fixed his eyes eagerly on the hole. 'Buried treasure,' he said. 'Diamonds or doubloons.'

Constable Elliot laughed.

The sergeant said, 'Whatever it is, I hardly think that it will be either of those. He might, after all, have been burying something, and not had time to finish the job.' He smiled at Ellie. 'Perhaps he was planting your chrysanthemum.'

The constable began to dig, placing the soil in small tidy heaps around the edge of the hole. He didn't have to dig for long. The spade caught, and twisted in his hands. He probed with his fingers and took a firm grip on a piece of old sacking which was just beneath the surface.

Roger knelt beside him and dug with both hands as the policeman eased the bundle from the soil. It came out quite willingly, and trickles of earth ran from the folds as he hoisted it up. The mouth of the sack was not secured in any way, but simply folded over.

The sergeant took it from him and bent to open it and let the sunlight in. No one else moved at all.

'Ah,' he said. 'Well, well!'

The three others stepped simultaneously towards him, but he closed the top of the sack and smiled vaguely at the beech-tree with his head on one side.

Ellie pulled at his sleeve.

'May we see?' she said.

The sergeant didn't answer but carried the sack out of the shadow into the full sunlight and picked up the black rug, which Ellie had folded neatly and placed beside the path. He handed it to her.

'Open it out, will you, please, and spread it on the grass,' he said.

When she had done this he picked up the sack by the two bottom corners, and gently tumbled the contents out on to the rug.

It was not Spanish gold, nor yet diamonds. Every piece was silver. A little bowl with birds and flowers exquisitely engraved within it rolled over and came to rest near Ellie's feet. She knelt and stretched her hand towards it.

'No,' said the sergeant at once. 'Nothing must be touched at all.'

He raised his side of the rug and shook it a little to spread the pieces out. There were salvers and shallow dishes of various sizes, a snuff box with a rose on the lid, small slender candle-sticks elegantly decorated with tiny leaves, heavy candle-sticks unpatterned, and more bowls, but none as beautiful as the one beside Ellie.

'Twenty-five pieces,' declared the sergeant. 'Check, please.'

The constable and Ellie agreed with him, and so did Roger after a recount.

'That's correct then,' said the sergeant in a satisfied voice. 'There's nothing missing.'

'Is this the silver from the house?' asked Roger.

The sergeant nodded and looked at his watch.

'Is Mr Maitland at home, do you know?' he asked.

'No,' said Ellie. 'Mrs Simkin told me that he is in Scotland, and Mrs Bassett, his housekeeper, is on holiday too.'

'Well, we must get back to Riddington straight away,' said the sergeant. 'Inspector Charles will certainly be pleased to see us! We can bring B.P. down for a sniff around, and then call on you for your statement, Miss Leyland. We'll let you know how Mr Simkin is.'

They went back up the ride to the car. The sergeant and Constable Elliot carried the silver between them, swaying gently in the black hammock of the car-rug. Ellie carried the sack, and Roger carried the spade, holding it gingerly by the metal shaft. The silver was placed reverently in the back of the car, and Ellie and Roger sat on the edge of the seat, being very careful not to lean against it.

'Crikey,' said Roger, looking at his watch. 'This is going to be more like high tea than dinner.'

Ellie didn't answer, because she didn't hear him. She was looking at the flowers engraved within the little bowl, apple-blossom and forget-me-nots. She was thinking of the forgotten man who had made it, and the vanished houses that had sheltered it, and the dead hands that had held it, long ago.

14

Cat and Mouse

'MY GOODNESS ME, Roger!' exclaimed Daddy. He was sitting on the window-seat in the kitchen. 'Your capacity for food seems to be never failing, like the widow's cruse of oil.'

'Marmalade is one of my favourite foods,' said Roger, skilfully eating a slice of bread which positively sagged under the weight of it.

'Marmalade is one of my favourite words,' said Ellie. She held the pot up so that the sunlight glowed in it. 'Marmmmalade. Maaarmalade.'

'Oh, you are dippy,' said Roger. 'You waste altogether too much time on words. Eating's the thing.'

'It certainly seems to be with you, anyway,' said Mother, clearing the table round him. 'Hurry up now. I want to finish the washing-up before the police arrive, and then it will soon be time for tea. Today has been nothing but one long meal for me. I shall have to live on vitamin pills soon, like pilots in rubber dinghies, because the sight of food will make me sick.'

Roger pushed the remainder of the slice into his mouth and went reluctantly upstairs to wash his hands. Mother emptied the tepid washing-up water away, and began again with fresh hot water from the kettle. Ellie dried for her.

Jane was still busy in the apple-tree. Although she had

intended her house to be like the round nest of a harvest-mouse, it was turning out to be rather more like that of a magpie, an haphazard and untidy collection of sticks and dead leaves. She was keeping a careful eye on the back

door, so that she would see when the police arrived. She felt that she had missed a large share of the excitement so far, and was determined not to miss any more.

A black car drew up by the gate and two policemen got out. They stood for a moment in the road looking at the front of the house while the car reversed smoothly and turned, to go back the way it had come through the village. Jane saw them, slithered down from the tree, and ran up the lawn with dead leaves in her hair and green tree-stains on her hands and knees. She arrived at the back door just before they did, and burst into the kitchen shouting, 'They've come!'

The taller of the two men smiled as he rapped on the open door and walked straight in.

'I see that we are expected,' he said. 'I am Inspector Charles, and this is Sergeant Buchan whom the young lady and gentleman have met already this morning.'

'How is Mr Simkin?' asked Ellie.

'Where's B.P.?' asked Jane.

'Have you had any dinner?' asked Roger.

'Now then,' said Mother. 'You are supposed to answer questions, not to ask them. You come upstairs with me, Jane, and I'll endeavour to make you clean and tidy again.' She turned to the two policemen. 'Do sit down. Would you like a cup of tea in a few moments?'

'Thank you, Mrs Leyland. Whenever it is convenient for you,' said Inspector Charles.

Sergeant Buchan leant across the table to Ellie.

'Mr Simkin is very much better now,' he said quietly. 'He'll probably come home tomorrow morning.'

'Thank you,' said Ellie. She wondered why the sergeant looked somehow different this afternoon, and then realized that it was because he was no longer in command, but only an assistant to Inspector Charles.

The inspector sat back in the old basket-chair, and carefully crossed one leg over the other. The chair sighed to itself and creaked as it settled down.

'Now, Ellie,' he said. 'Can you tell me briefly what happened this morning after you turned off the main ride into the wood? Sergeant Buchan will take it down as you tell me and then we shan't have to trouble you again. Not too fast, mind. How's your shorthand these days, Sergeant?'

'It's a little hesitant at the moment, Sir,' he said. 'But I'll let you know if you go too quickly for me.'

Ellie sat down on the hearth-rug, since all the comfortable chairs were occupied, and did as he asked. Afterwards she described the two previous occasions on which she and Roger had seen the Mouse-man in Tambley.

'And,' she concluded, 'I think that it is he who cuts holes in our front window in the middle of the night, but nobody else does.'

'Ah, now why should you think that? Did anyone see anything of the man?' asked Inspector Charles. He turned to Roger.

'No,' he said. 'I nearly did. I was almost at the bottom of the stairs when Angus started to bark and frightened him off.'

Then Roger had to describe how he had heard the squeaks in the middle of the night, and looked down from his bedroom window at the man standing beneath him in the garden.

'Did he have a hat on?' asked the inspector.

'Yes,' said Roger. 'A trilby. I did a lovely stalk down the stairs. I would have seen the whole of him through the window if it hadn't been for Angus.'

Mother came downstairs then, and crossed over to put the kettle on. Angus stepped out of his box because he heard his name mentioned, and walked stiff-legged round Ellie on the hearth-rug to stretch himself, dragging each back leg in turn and yawning squeakily.

Jane looked over Sergeant Buchan's shoulder to see what he had put down in his note-book.

'Your writing's not very good,' she said. 'I can't read it.'

'Come over here, Jane, and fill the sugar basin for me,' said Mother. 'That's shorthand and not writing at all.'

Jane didn't mean to be diverted this time.

'Where is B.P.?' she asked. 'I want to see him. I've never seen a police-dog. Do they have a number on their collar?'

Inspector Charles smiled at her, and reached down for his brief-case beside the chair.

'B.P. is down in the wood, finding out some more things about this Mouse-man for us. I've been down there myself with Sergeant Buchan, but we can't find out anything else just by ourselves. You will see him in a little while, because they are all coming up in the car to fetch us, when they are ready,' he said. 'I hope that we shall not be in your way here, Mrs Leyland. They shouldn't be very much longer down there. The man seems to have been paddling to and fro across the river. I don't think that they will hold the trail for long.'

He rummaged about in the brief-case and drew out a flat tin, which he handed across to Ellie.

'Did you drop this, this morning?' he asked. 'B.P. found it for us, just by the hole.'

Ellie looked at the tin in astonishment.

'No,' she said. 'Daddy won't let me smoke a pipe, yet. It's more likely to be Mr Simkin's.'

The policemen laughed, and Roger and Jane and Daddy went to look at it too. The tin had at one time held tobacco which it guaranteed as being full and mellow, satisfying to any taste. The inspector took it back and twisted off the lid.

'Sorry,' he said. 'I really meant this.'

He found a pair of small tweezers in his pocket and took out of the tin a tight roll of paper which he laid on the kitchen table. He unrolled it and held it flat with two matchsticks. Everyone except Sergeant Buchan crowded round him to see what it was.

'Some sort of plan,' said Daddy.

'I see what it is,' said Roger. 'It's a kind of diagram of that part of the wood. There's the river, and there's the ride.'

'And there's that enormous beech-tree,' said Ellie. 'No one could miss that. Those squiggles must mean the little trees and bushes in the clearing. The old beech rises straight out of the middle of them.'

'That's right,' said the inspector. 'But the most important thing is here, this little circle.'

'The hole,' said Roger.

'Yes.' The inspector took the matchsticks away and the paper immediately rolled up on itself, as though trying to keep its secret. It was returned to the tobacco tin with the tweezers and put back into the brief-case.

'But if the Mouse-man stole the silver from the Hall in the first place, why did he need a plan to know where to dig it up again?' asked Ellie.

'Perhaps he thought he would forget where he'd put it,' said Roger.

'How silly,' said Jane.

Mother put the tea-pot on the table and fetched scones and chocolate biscuits from the pantry.

'Could you give us a brief description of this Mouse-man, as you call him, Ellie?' asked the inspector. 'We shall need it for circulation.'

'He really does look like a mouse,' she said. 'White and quivery.'

'Do you mean absolutely white, like an albino? Did he have pink eyes?' asked Sergeant Buchan.

'Oh, I've only ever seen a white blackbird,' said Ellie. 'I didn't know there were human albinos.'

The inspector nodded. 'Yes, but he isn't one?'

'No,' said Ellie. 'At least, he hasn't got pink eyes. He is about as tall as Mother, but not so fat. His hands are very thin and the veins stand out on them. His wrist bones stick out too; I noticed that especially because the sleeve of his pullover was coming undone at the cuff. He's got very blond hair that is very smooth against his head, and then he has a long thin nose and a receding chin. His eyes are a pale grey, and his eyelashes and eyebrows are as blond as his hair, so you can see that he does truly look like a mouse.'

'Yes, indeed he must do. That's a very clear description of him, Ellie,' said Inspector Charles. He turned to Roger. 'Would you agree with that?'

'Well, as far as I know it's about right,' said Roger. 'But it was late when I saw him, almost lighting-up time, so I can't really be sure.'

'I see,' said the inspector. 'Well, we must have that description sent round to all regions as soon as possible, and radioed to all cars. If he tries to move out of this area, I don't think he'll get far, but if he has a lie-up somewhere near by, it may be more difficult.'

He began to discuss the new police headquarters in Bewley then, and it was just after Mother had emptied the tea-pot that a policeman knocked on the back door. Roger went to open it. It was the driver who had brought Angus back yesterday. The inspector looked at his watch and stood up.

'Thank you for your help, and for the tea, Mrs Leyland,' he said. 'We must get straight back now. If anyone would like to see B.P., I expect he will be in the car.'

Everyone did, and he was. Constable Elliot was sitting

in the seat beside the driver's, and B.P. sat on newspapers on the floor between his legs. The inspector opened the door so that Jane could see him better.

'I don't think I should allow him out, Sir, if I were you,' said Constable Elliot. 'He's very wet and muddy because he's been climbing in and out of the river ever since you left us. It was a good thing that we brought the waders with us.'

B.P. swished his tail on the newspapers as Jane cautiously patted him.

'He looks a very sensible dog,' she said.

'Yes, indeed he is,' said the inspector. 'Did you have any luck, Elliot?'

'Not really, Sir. We got down below the chicken-farm, but then he seemed to have walked straight up the river and we lost him completely. We really upset that big Alsatian that is chained in the farmyard. B.P. was half inclined to run up and have a chat.'

Jane rubbed the big police-dog behind the ears to say good-bye, while Inspector Charles and Sergeant Buchan got into the back seat. The three doors slammed at the same time and the car drew quietly away.

'Tea-time,' said Roger. 'All this excitement is good for my appetite.'

'It is funny,' said Ellie, 'how some days fly past and you've no sooner got up than you're going to bed, but how other days seem to go on for weeks. It seems ages since we had porridge with cream for breakfast.'

'Yes,' said Mother. 'It does, and you never got me any haws.'

15

Trapped!

SUNDAY MORNING WAS wet and windy, and the clouds were low over Highcomb. No one went to church as they had to share their Vicar with Sneeton-under-Hill, and this week it was Tambley's turn for Evensong. Roger went off straight after breakfast to Hudsons', to do some more boat-building. Ellie and Jane took Angus for a walk down by the river, and dawdled home because of the potato-peeling which waited for them.

When they got back, Jane dried Angus and combed the mud out of his hair. Ellie was combing the mud out of Jane's hair when someone knocked at the back door. It was Sergeant Buchan.

'Hello, again,' he said, when Ellie opened it. 'Is your mother or father at home?'

'Yes,' said Ellie. 'Will you come in? Mother's upstairs and Daddy's round in the garage. Shall I call Mother?'

'No, don't trouble her,' said Sergeant Buchan. 'You go on with what you are doing, and I'll go and see your father. I can find my own way.'

He could hardly have lost it, because Mr Leyland was singing *Heart of Oak* at the top of his voice and sawing the legs off the old bureau at the same time. The sawing and the singing stopped abruptly. Five minutes later, the two of them came into the kitchen together.

'Sergeant Buchan wants to take you for a ride, Ellie,' said Daddy. 'They think that they have caught your Mouse-man, and Inspector Charles would be very pleased if you would go over to Riddington and make sure for them. Mr Simkin is going with you.'

Ellie nodded and went through to fetch her coat. Jane ran upstairs to let Mother know.

'Where did they find him, then?' asked Ellie.

'Getting on for Gloucester,' said the sergeant. 'He'd made good time. He seems to have been making his way over to Bristol, and there's plenty of lorry traffic giving lifts on that road.'

'Will she be back in time for dinner?' asked Mother.

'Oh, yes, it'll not take very long,' said Sergeant Buchan. 'We'll pick Mr Simkin up at the hospital on our way, and then I'll bring them both back to Tambley afterwards.'

They all went to the gate, and watched the car go down through the village. Ellie waved through the back window.

'It's not fair,' said Jane. 'I'm missing all the fun, and now I've got to peel the potatoes on my own.'

'Never mind,' said Daddy, 'I'll help you with them, just this once.'

Ellie hoped that they might meet Roger on his way up from Hudsons', but they didn't. Turning left at the cross-roads, they soon passed Bewley Grammar School and drew up at the hospital farther down the High Street.

'Shan't be long,' said Sergeant Buchan. 'I expect that Mr Simkin will be ready for us.'

Ellie sat and looked at the Sunday-empty street, and wondered if she'd have to go down to the cells to see the Mouse-man, and spy at him through a little hole in the door. Then she was pleased to see two girls passing on the opposite pavement stop and stare at her in amazement and curiosity, before walking on. They were both in the fourth form at Riddington High School.

'That'll give them something to talk about,' said Ellie to herself.

The hospital door opened and Mr Simkin came out, with Sergeant Buchan behind him carrying his suitcase. Mr Simkin opened the rear door and got in.

'Well, Ellie girl,' he said. 'And how's yourself? I've been hearing all sorts of yarns from Mrs Simkin. Came in again last evening to see me, and tells me as you and Roger helped the police to dig up all the boss's silver. Got the story from Arthur, she says.'

'Yes,' said Ellie, 'I suppose that is partly true, except that Roger and I didn't help exactly. We just watched. How is your head now?'

'Oh, it'd take a sledgehammer, let alone a spade, to do much damage to that,' said Mr Simkin, taking the suitcase from Sergeant Buchan over the front seat. 'Solid bone, that is.'

The sergeant turned the car in the hospital yard and went back down the High Street to Riddington.

'I'll leave the car outside the station,' he said. 'Then it will be ready to get you back in time for dinner. I went up to tell Mrs Simkin what time to expect us before I collected Ellie. She seemed to have a houseful.'

'That'll be Frank and Nellie and their family,' said Mr Simkin. 'I'd forgotten all about them. I shall be able to make their hair curl now, shan't I, Ellie?'

They turned up Pippin Street to the police-station, and stopped by the front door. Ellie saw a head bob up over the half-curtain to see who it was. Inspector Charles opened the door just as they reached it.

'I'm very pleased to see you both,' he said. 'I've got rather a restive crowd on my hands in the back room, all beginning to feel hungry. Come through here, will you?'

He led the way along a yellow-brown corridor that smelt of soap, into a small waiting-room. It reminded Ellie immediately of her dentist. There was a row of hard chairs ranged coldly along one wall, and an equally hard shiny leather settee against another. Instead of the dentist's *Keep Smiling* which hung over his fire-place, here there was a dusty notice which informed her that Colorado beetles were still to be met with and must be escorted at once to the nearest police-station.

Inspector Charles saw her looking round, and switched on the electric fire.

'That might make it a little more cheerful,' he said. 'But you won't be in here long enough to get morbid depression. I think I'll take Mr Simkin in first. I captured five men out of the street about a quarter of an hour ago, and the suspect Mouse-man is in with them. I just want you each to walk through the room with me, and then to tell me what you think. I only hope that you don't both fasten on to one of the five innocent citizens now anxious for their Sunday dinner, that's all!'

The door shut behind him and Mr Simkin, and Ellie went over to the window. The police car-park and garages were outside, and she saw a man on a bicycle turn in from the road pedalling with his heels and looking every inch a policeman, although he was not in uniform. He left his bicycle in the rack and disappeared round the corner of the building. A grimy tennis ball rolled in from the street then, and was followed after a short interval by an equally grimy small boy. Someone knocked on the window in the room next to the waiting-room, and the boy seized the ball and scuttled out of the yard as if the Commissioner himself were after him.

Ellie walked back to the electric fire to warm her hands, and studied the Colorado beetle picture on the poster. It looked rather like the burying-beetle that she had seen last summer walking pensively across the back of a dead sparrow, measuring it with its eye. That was the first burying-beetle that she had seen, and she had been surprised to find that a beetle which led such a depressing life could look so smart and cheerful.

The door opened and Inspector Charles came in, followed by Mr Simkin.

'I've not to speak to you, Ellie,' said Mr Simkin. 'So I won't.'

Inspector Charles smiled and held the door open for her. She followed him a little farther down the corridor and into a large room in which six men stood in a row and Constable Elliot sat at a large desk.

Ellie walked quickly down the line. As soon as she entered the room she had seen the Mouse-man, standing at the far end. When she stopped in front of him, she saw that his hands were shaking and his eyes fixed despairingly on the wall above her head.

'I'm sorry,' she said.

He looked down at her and straightened himself.

'Never mind, Miss,' he said, and seemed relieved that the waiting was over. 'Did the little dog get back safe?'

'Yes, thank you,' said Ellie.

'I think that we need not keep you any longer, gentlemen,' said Inspector Charles, opening the door. 'Thank you for your co-operation.'

The five men hurried away, and Ellie followed them out.

'I'll be with you in just a few minutes,' said the inspector.

The door closed behind her. She walked quickly down the corridor and into the waiting-room. Mr Simkin looked up from the Colorado beetle.

'I'd know one of these creatures anywhere now,' he said. 'Even if I only saw it for half a second in a thick fog. They don't leave you much to take your mind off things here, do they?'

Ellie moved a hard chair over to the electric fire, and sat on the edge of it.

'Did you remember him?' she asked. 'Did you tell Inspector Charles which man it was?'

'Oh, yes, I remembered him well enough,' said Mr Simkin, patting the strip of sticking-plaster on the top of his head.

'Whatever he has done,' said Ellie, 'I feel almost sorry for him. He looks so miserable. He admitted that he did take Angus away; he asked me if he got home safely.'

'Well I'll be jiggered!' said Mr Simkin. 'That must mean you were right then, about him being the breaker-and-enterer.'

'Yes,' said Ellie. 'I wish I could see why, though. It all seems very disconnected at the moment.'

'Here's the sergeant,' said Mr Simkin. 'Putting the car away, he is. I hope he remembers he's got my best pyjamas in the back of it.'

Ellie turned to the window in time to see the police car disappear into the garage opposite. Sergeant Buchan opened the rear door and took out Mr Simkin's case, then pulled the garage doors together and closed the padlock. He smiled at them, waving the case in the air, and then pointed across the yard to an old green Riley on the other side. He walked over to it, got in, and drove out of the yard.

As Ellie was beginning to wonder if they were, after all, going to get home in time for dinner, the door opened and Inspector Charles came in.

'Sorry to keep you hanging about for so long,' he said. 'But I had to get the Mouse-man settled down. You may be disappointed, Ellie, but he has quite an ordinary name—Michael Robinson.'

'Oh, what a shame,' said Ellie. 'I expected something like Uriah Heep or Cyril Slime. We have just seen Sergeant Buchan putting the car away. Have we to stay longer?'

'No, but he's off duty now, so I told him that I'd take you up to Tambley myself. It's on my way, more or less, because I live on this side of Bewley. Come along, now; I'm sure you've been in this room long enough. We aren't being redecorated because we've grown out of this building, and so we're having a new divisional headquarters built in Bewley. Be handy for me, of course, and it's a good site there, too.'

He opened the front door and the Riley was waiting for them outside.

'I do like these old cars much better than the new ones that have horrible expressions,' said Ellie. 'They always seem to leer at you, whereas these either look kind or cheerful or dignified.'

The inspector and Mr Simkin laughed at her.

'Well, I suppose that engines and suspension are more important in the long run,' said Inspector Charles. 'But I do know what you mean.'

They went past Ellie's school and left Riddington by the Bewley road.

'The Mouse-man did take Angus away then,' said Ellie. 'So I was half right, wasn't I?'

'You were completely right, as it happens,' replied the inspector. 'It must have been that peculiar feminine intuition.'

'Can you fill in the pieces that I can't understand, please?' asked Ellie.

'Yes, I think I may be able to,' he said. 'I had a telegram from Mr Maitland half an hour ago, and he's calling on me this afternoon, otherwise I shouldn't really do so before he returned. It's really quite a simple explanation, once you've had it explained to you. It usually is. Before I forget, please remind me to ask you to lend me one of the remaining wooden chrysanthemums before I go back.'

As the old Riley ran quietly along the road towards the river and the hill, the inspector filled in the gaps for Ellie, and Mr Simkin sat forward in his seat to listen. They both arrived in time for dinner, and Inspector Charles returned to the Bewley cross-roads with one pink chrysanthemum on the seat beside him.

16

I Told You So

ELLIE HAD RUSHED in for the chrysanthemum and rushed out again without any explanation. When she opened the door for the second time, she was pleased to see her dinner and her audience ready and waiting for her.

'I knew it,' said Daddy. 'Almost smug. Almost self-satisfied. You were right all the time? Please accept our abject apologies.'

'Blow!' said Roger. 'Go on, say it!'

'Say what?' asked Ellie, trying to stop herself smiling, but without success.

'I told you so,' said Roger. 'Women are always saying it.'

'But I haven't said it,' objected Ellie. 'And I wasn't going to, either. Still, you must admit that you all laughed at me. Anyway, how do you know that I was right all the time?'

'Your face, for one thing,' said Mother, setting the gravy down on the table.

'Taking a chrysanthemum for the inspector for another,' said Daddy. 'We can't see how it has any connexion with the Hall's silver, though. Are you going to tell us?'

'Sit down,' said Jane. 'And you can have some of my potatoes. I dug them out of the garden; I peeled them; I mashed them. They are mine, but you can have some if you like.'

'Thank you,' said Ellie. 'Well, shall I start at what we

136

understand and go backwards, or shall I start at the beginning?'

'Start your dinner,' said Mother.

'At the beginning,' said Roger.

'That's silly,' said Jane. 'She could hardly eat her dinner from the end first.'

Finally, the story had to wait until after dinner entirely. It had, of course, to be a monologue since no one else knew anything about it, and the gravy on Ellie's plate began to settle under a thin film of grease.

'Now I don't want to hear another word about it until everyone has finished and the washing-up has been done,' said Mother firmly.

Jane, Roger, and Daddy ate fast and furiously after this, and had begun to wash up whilst Mother and Ellie were still eating their pudding. Jane skipped to and fro, putting the things away as soon as Roger placed them on the table. Ellie put down her spoon with a sigh of satisfaction and found the plate immediately whisked away.

'Hmnn,' said Mother, 'I must think about this carefully. I seem to be on to a good thing.'

Her plate disappeared as she spoke and the tablecloth leapt up from the table and hurried out of the door, accompanied by Roger.

'There, that's much better,' she said. 'Now you can begin at the beginning, Ellie.'

'Very well,' said Ellie, and went to sit on the table. 'Are you all sitting comfortably?'

'Come on, come on,' said Daddy, and padded down the tobacco with his thumb before lighting his pipe. His hair fell forward as he struck the match, and he lit his hair instead.

Mother jumped up and put it out before it had properly begun to burn, by clutching Daddy's forelock in a chair-back.

'I told you so,' she said, and sat down rather suddenly on his knee. 'You're even more stupid than Roger is about having a hair-cut. That piece at the front is practically long enough to plait.'

'Was, you mean,' said Ellie, gently pulling the charred ends away. 'You'll have to have a hair-cut now.'

'You look as if the moths have been at you, Daddy,' said Jane.

'You see, I was right,' said Roger. ' "I told you so." Women always *are* saying it.'

Daddy finally lit his pipe while holding his chin up and his pipe down. Ellie began again.

'The Mouse-man has a name,' she said. 'It's Michael Robinson.'

'Mickey Mouse,' said Roger.

'He also has a cousin,' said Ellie. 'And he's the villain of the piece, really, and not poor Mouse-man at all.'

'Good,' said Jane. 'I like Mickey Mouse.'

'And the cousin,' continued Ellie, 'is Jack Armstrong.'

'Jack Armstrong!' exclaimed Daddy. 'But he lived in Tambley nearly all his life!'

'Yes,' said Ellie. 'And that's why he *is* the villain.'

'I remember him,' said Roger. 'Phil Donald's wife is his sister, isn't she?'

Philip Donald was one of Mr Kennedy's farm workers, and a great friend of Roger's.

'Yes, that's right,' said Mother. 'Anne Armstrong she was, and lived with her father until he died. It must be three years since Jack left home.'

'It is,' said Ellie. 'And he's been in prison for almost two of them, in Bristol. I expect that poor Mr Armstrong was too ashamed to talk about it.'

'He always was a bad boy. It seemed to be in his nature,' said Mother. 'Such a pity, because they were a nice family. Go on, Ellie.'

'I'm trying to,' she said, looking frustrated. 'If you will all keep quiet for just ten minutes, I can tell you the whole story from beginning to end.'

They sat obediently silent, looking up at her and waiting for her to begin.

'Oh, I forgot,' she said apologetically. 'I haven't my important piece of evidence with me now. Will you fetch it for me, Roger, as you're nearest to the door? I shall need a wooden chrysanthemum.'

Jane wriggled in expectation of some excitement.

He brought her through a yellow one, and she sat on the table and twirled it in her fingers.

'Now,' she said. 'Please do let me tell it straight through, or I shall be muddled up. Jack Armstrong lived with his family at what is now Mr Hudson's chicken-farm, just below the Hall. He was on probation for the first time soon after he was ten, and by the time he left home at twenty was well known to the police in the Bewley area. He found farming too much like hard work, and went down to Bristol, where he had an uncle. He didn't settle there for long but joined up with his cousin, Mickey Mouse the Mouse-man. They had an old lorry and travelled round doing odd days of labouring work. A few months ago they were travelling in company with some hybrid gipsies, which is when he got the idea of using a wooden chrysanthemum.'

'What are hybrid gipsies, for goodness' sake?' asked Daddy.

'Oh, the scruffy tinkery sort that Mr Simkin calls Didikaies,' said Ellie. 'Not proper Romanies.'

'Using a wooden chrysanthemum for what?' asked Roger. 'Come on. Cut the cackle.'

'I can't be any quicker,' said Ellie. 'To put it in a nutshell, Jack Armstrong made up his mind to take the silver from the Hall. He knew that Mr Maitland was away very often, and he knew about how much it was worth. He was sure that he could get in without disturbing anyone, but realized that he wouldn't be able to carry the silver very far. He also realized that he couldn't take any vehicle up the drive, or even up the lane, to collect it, because of Mr Simkin's dogs, and Sam roaming about on the chicken-farm. Also, he was so well known in the district that if he was seen here, the police would automatically take him for questioning.'

'The chrysanthemum,' said Jane, bobbing in her chair. 'Get to the chrysanthemum.'

'All right, all right,' said Ellie, tapping her on the head with the yellow one. 'Well, what Jack planned to do was this: he was to steal the silver, carry it as far into the woodland as he could, and then bury it carefully. There were plenty of dead leaves to hide the place with, of course. Then he sent a diagram of its position off to the Mouse-man, who had only to sit tight for several months and then to collect it at his leisure to dispose of it after the alert had died down. Jack himself went immediately over to Ireland to be out of the way for a while.'

'So far so good,' said Daddy. 'What went wrong?'

'The little plan showing the position of the hole went missing on its way to the Mouse-man,' said Ellie. 'Mickey Mouse was waiting in Bewley, but Jack had to get out of the area before the morning. He sent the plan by a gipsy, who knew them both, and thought it would be quite safe.'

'And the gipsy tried to run away with it?' suggested Mother.

'No,' said Ellie. 'The gipsy didn't know that he'd been given a plan at all. Jack simply asked him to give a bronze chrysanthemum to the Mouse-man. They had used a wooden chrysanthemum before to pass a message to each other. Look.'

She pulled the head of the yellow chrysanthemum from the twig that made the stem. 'There's just room here, if the head is made especially loose, to fit in a roll of paper. Jack put the little plan in here, in a bronze chrysanthemum, and gave it to the gipsy to be delivered. It was cash on delivery, so he knew that the Mouse-man would get it. The trouble was that the gipsy had a whole basketful of his own chry-santhemums to sell, and couldn't resist making three and threepence by selling us seven when he met us on his way to Bewley. He had pushed the bronze one Jack gave him under the paper at the bottom of the basket, and thought that it would be safe there. Someone took it.'

Jane twisted her legs together in her excitement, and leant forward to look solemnly up at Mother.

'I did,' she said, in a hushed voice. 'I took it out.'

'Oh, Jane!' said Mother. 'Wicked one.'

'We thought it had just slipped under by accident, and it was better than the others,' said Ellie. 'When the gipsy went to get it out to give it to the Mouse-man, of course it wasn't there. They thought it must have slipped out and be loose in the basket with the rest. The Mouse-man took the head off every bronze chrysanthemum in the basket, but found no message. Then the gipsy realized what had happened. All he knew about us was that we lived in Castle Tambley. There you are—the rest you know.'

'So the Mouse-man had to cut two holes in our window *and* kidnap Angus before he even knew where to dig for the silver,' said Daddy.

'Poor soul,' said Mother. 'I wonder if he'll get away with being an accessory after the fact, or if it will be a joint charge.'

'And then in the end, it was only coincidence that you and Mr Simkin disturbed him,' said Roger. 'He might have got clear away.'

'Inspector Charles thinks that they would have caught him, anyway,' said Ellie. 'He didn't wait long enough, you see. They were still keeping a strict watch on the dealers. It was only two months and four days after the actual theft, but all the worry of getting the bronze chrysanthemum away from us shattered his nerves!'

'Thank goodness I knew nothing of this before,' said Mother. 'We've been living in the middle of a mystery.'

'Dumbfounded and flabbergasted, I am,' said Daddy.

'Flabbergasted,' echoed Jane.

'Well, I'm jolly pleased,' said Roger. 'Do you realize that Simon Wilkins was wrong for once? There isn't a Saxon treasure-cache buried under the foundations. He'll be so annoyed!'

17

Cleaning It All Up

A WEEK LATER Mr Maitland asked the three of them to go up to the Hall for tea. Mrs Bassett, his housekeeper, came round after church with the message, wearing her best black and the hat with the autumn hatband on. She had only the one hat and wore it every Sunday until it reached that state when only suitable to be handed down to her niece Emily, housemaid at The Elms, Bewley. The hatband changed with the four seasons, but the hat itself was always grey, a little more grey than her hair. The autumn hatband was dark red.

Mrs Leyland accepted on their behalf, since they had all gone out for a walk up the hill before dinner. She was a little apprehensive about doing so, because she knew that Roger would object, for one, and that all of them would regard it rather more as an ordeal than as a pleasure.

Mr Maitland was hardly known in the village. He was a keen archaeologist and was away for much of the year, helping at various excavations. He also had a small estate in Scotland which took up some of his time. Consequently, only his employees knew anything about him. Mr Simkin had spoken of him to Ellie sometimes. He liked and respected him because he understood trees and animals as well as he did himself; Mrs Simkin liked and respected him because he always raised his hat to her and sent in a brace of pheasants when he had been shooting.

It was raining again before they reached home and they had all got their hair wet. Mother told them of Mr Maitland's invitation while she was drying Jane's.

'I can't go,' said Roger. 'The river will be frozen to a depth of forty feet before we get that boat on it, at the rate we're going.'

'I'm sorry, but I do think that you ought to,' said Mother. 'After all, it will be nice to know that you are the only villagers outside the estate who have seen inside the Hall. In any case, I've accepted now and so you have to.'

'He'll probably have a stuffed dinosaur on the landing and a mammoth's head hung in the library,' said Daddy. 'Seize your opportunities, boy. You can build boats any day.'

'I suppose that's true,' said Roger. 'And we can call in at Hudsons' on our way up.'

'But mammoths are bigger than elephants, aren't they? And all hairy too,' said Jane. 'I don't want to go.'

'Don't believe a word that your father said. There won't be an animal in the house larger than his labrador,' said Mother consolingly. 'All he'll have to show for his diggings will be little chips off Romans' second best tea-sets, and a Saxon slipper or two that a Saxon dog chewed.'

'Well,' said Ellie, 'I'm going, if no one else is. I want to see the silver when it's all been cleaned.'

'I don't suppose that it will be on view,' said Roger. 'He most likely keeps it locked away in some dusty old strong-box and never looks at it from one year's end to the next.'

'Now you see that you have to go, if only to find out who's right,' said Mother. 'But anyway, there's no question of your not going. It is most kind of him to ask you. After all, you didn't do anything to recover his silver—you just happened to be there.'

'Yes, all right,' said Roger. 'But all this talk about tea has made me want my dinner. Isn't it ready yet?'

They set off as soon as they could afterwards, because the chain on Jane's bicycle was broken and they had to walk.

'Perhaps it's just as well,' said Daddy. 'Because I think that it will rain again before long. Now Mr Coles or Mr Simkin will probably be asked to give you a lift home.'

'I hope we don't come with Mr Simkin,' said Jane. 'He has ferrets in that van, and I'm frightened of them.'

'He doesn't have them in at the same time as people, though,' said Ellie.

'Doesn't he?' said Jane, and sounded unconvinced.

Roger went down through the Hudsons' farm buildings to find Eggo and Peter, whilst Ellie and Jane walked on slowly towards the Hall. The sun was still shining, but a low bank of cloud was advancing steadily towards it. Cloud shadows swooped silently over the hill, and the raindrops hanging in rows on the bare brown twigs hung grey and dull one moment and the next shone and sparkled like diamonds.

They were watching a thrush looking for snails in the woodside when Roger caught up with them. He tapped on the lodge window as they went past but Mr Simkin was out.

The drive curving gracefully up to the house was bordered with large white stones set beneath a holly hedge. The house itself was hidden by the shrubbery, and they came upon it quite suddenly.

'Should we go round to the back door?' asked Roger.

'No,' said Ellie. 'We are Mr Maitland's guests. We're not going to have tea in the kitchen.'

'I wish we were,' said Jane.

The front of the house was covered with Virginia creeper, and even the window-sills were hidden by it.

'This is pretty. I wish we could have some at home,' said Ellie, looking at the bright leaves trembling in the wind.

'Earwigs,' said Roger. 'Great armies of them, climbing through your bedroom window every night.'

Ellie stood and considered the front door for a moment. There was a large bell-pull which looked as if it could rouse the entire village, if necessary. There was an enormous brass knocker in the shape of a lion's head with a ring in its mouth, and there was a small green bell-button, which looked as if it would shine in the dark. Ellie decided on this, and pressed it twice.

They heard a door open, and quick footsteps tapping along a bare stone corridor; then sudden silence as they came to the carpet of the hall. Mrs Bassett herself opened the door and stood smiling at them.

'Come in, my dears,' she said. 'You've just managed to arrive before the rain does.'

They went into a square hall, and Ellie was relieved to see that there were no stuffed heads of any kind on the walls. She saw Jane looking too.

Mrs Bassett led the way into a very large sitting-room with a very small fire burning in the grate.

'Sit down and be comfortable,' she said. 'Mr Maitland told me to take you to his study, but really he's made such a mess in there, perhaps he's changed his mind. I'll go and see. I shan't be long.'

'It's all very well to say—"Sit down and be comfortable",' said Roger. 'It's just not possible on these chairs, let alone with all these eyes looking at you.'

The chairs were old and lovely, with faded brocade upholstery and gilded legs; they were also very, very hard. The eyes belonged to some twenty or so statues of various shapes and sizes which stood on every available surface in the room.

'Oh goodness!' said Ellie. 'I wouldn't like to have to dust in here.'

'I'm cold,' said Jane, 'I don't want to stay long.'

Mrs Bassett reappeared. 'I'm to take you to the study. Mr Maitland says he doesn't think you'll mind him being in a muddle.'

She trotted ahead of them through the hall and up a shallow flight of stairs.

She knocked on a pale blue door, said 'In you go!' and went on along the corridor.

Ellie heard a quiet voice say 'Come in!' and went in.

This room was light and airy, with a view over the park to the woodland, and was indeed in a muddle, a glorious muddle. A large oval table stood before an enormous fire, and was covered with the silver that Ellie and Roger had last seen lying on the back seat of the police car. Half of it was cleaned, and half of it wasn't. The wall-paper was the same blue as the door, but was almost hidden by book-shelves, photographs of mountains, old swords and pistols, maps, and cabinets containing pottery and glass.

Mr Maitland got up from a leather armchair by the fire, and came over to shake hands with them. He was tall and thin, with wild grey hair, but a young face beneath it.

'So you are the saviours of my silver,' he said. 'Come over and get warm.'

They found three stools waiting for them on the hearth-rug, and sat down.

'I didn't do anything at all,' said Jane. 'I missed every single piece of excitement.'

'We didn't really *do* anything,' said Roger. 'We were just there when things happened.'

'Never mind,' said Mr Maitland. 'I'm so pleased to have it back safely that I felt I must thank someone, and you aren't allowed to thank the police, you know. You won't mind if I finish doing this, will you?'

'Of course not,' said Ellie. 'May we help you?'

They sat and polished the silver until tea-time, and all talked as fast as they could. Mr Maitland told them about digging in Egypt and Spain, and the wild animals in Scotland, and the different sorts of dogs that he had had.

Jane was particularly interested in the latter, and Mr Maitland fetched a large book over for her to look at.

Bound handsomely in leather, it contained beautifully coloured illustrations of British dogs, with a page of information about each. She became completely engrossed in it.

Ellie told about her various meetings with the Mouseman, and Roger told about their boat-building in the shed on Mr Hudson's chicken-farm. Mr Maitland looked thoughtful then, and went over to rummage in a bureau by the window. He returned with a large key.

'Remind me to tell you about that before you go,' he said, putting it on the table.

He returned the silver then to its own cabinet, which stood against the wall opposite to the fire-place. The shelves were lined with deep crimson velvet, and the freshly polished silver brightly reflected the flames and the chimney-piece.

'You've won an argument for me, Mr Maitland,' said Ellie, smiling shyly at him. 'Roger thought that you would have your silver hidden away in a strong-box, but I was sure that you would want it to live with you, and to see it every day.'

'Oh, yes,' he replied. 'I'm afraid that I always keep any beautiful things near me, however valuable they may be. I suppose it is rather a temptation for any able burglar that happens to hear of it.'

Mrs Bassett brought in a tea which silenced even Roger for some time, and drew the curtains to shut out the rain. Afterwards, Jane politely reminded Mr Maitland about the key which still lay on the table.

'Ah, yes,' he said, and threw it across to Roger, who just managed to catch it. 'It's for you. Do you know the mostly derelict boat-house that stands where my woods go down to the Ridding?'

'Yes,' said Roger, 'it's not far from where the silver was buried.'

'That's right. The key is for that door. Inside, I hope you will find a very shabby three-seater canoe. If you can afford a tin of varnish and some spare time, you can be on the river next week.'

Roger stared at him in silence, and Mr Maitland turned to Jane.

'The book can be for you. See if you can find a Border terrier in it, to show me before you go.'

Ellie saw that it was to be left to her to make some protest at his generosity, but he didn't even listen to her. He got up and stood looking around the room in a considering kind of way, then crossed to the silver cabinet. He returned carrying the tiny bowl which had the apple-blossom and forget-me-nots engraved within it.

'This, if I am not mistaken,' he said, 'was originally intended for a lady's dressing-table. Will you keep it on yours for me, Ellie? I know that you will always love it and care for it.' He placed it in her lap.

'How did you know?' she asked. 'How did you know that I thought this more beautiful than anything?'

'It was easy,' he said, smiling down at her. 'You polished it at least four times!'

He was quite firm in his refusals to take back any of these gifts, and pointed out that they were all things that he wished taken care of, and trusted them to do so for him.

'You see,' he said, 'I am here for such a little time each year; I really feel that I am neglecting them myself. I shall be happy to know that you have them safe.'

It was considerably later than Jane's bed-time when he took them himself down the drive to the garage where

Mr Coles was getting the car out. The rain had gone, and the night was cold and clear. Thin clouds were streaming like smoke across the sky, and the ringed and frosty moon seemed to be sailing backwards through them. The holly hedge rustled in the wind.

They said good-bye to Mr Maitland and thanked him again in a way which left him in no doubt that his presents had been, and would be, appreciated.

Ellie and Roger sat in the back seat in the complete silence of their dreams as the car carried them quietly back home. Jane sat beside Mr Coles, holding her dog book carefully in her arms, and never stopped talking.